BONGO
FISHING

BonGo
FiSHiNG

THACHER HURD

HENRY HOLT AND COMPANY

NEW YORK

Thanks to Marissa, Elisa, Natacha,
Susan, Sam, Will, Abigail, Laurence,
Abbe, and always to Olivia

Henry Holt and Company, LLC
Publishers since 1866
175 Fifth Avenue
New York, New York 10010
mackids.com

Library of Congress Cataloging-in-Publication Data
Hurd, Thacher.
Bongo fishing / Thacher Hurd.—1st ed.
p. cm.
Summary: Berkeley, California, middle-schooler Jason Jameson has a
close encounter of the fun kind when Sam, a bluish alien from the Pleiades,
arrives in a 1960 Dodge Dart spaceship and invites Jason to go fishing.
ISBN 978-0-8050-9100-7 (hc : alk. paper)
[1. Extraterrestrial beings—Fiction. 2. Adventure and adventurers—Fiction.
3. Space flight—Fiction. 4. Family life—California—Fiction. 5. Berkeley (Calif.)—Fiction.
6. Humorous stories. 7. Science fiction.] I. Title.
PZ7.H9562Bon 2011 [Fic]—dc22 2010011696

First Edition—2011
Printed in December 2010 in the United States of America by
R. R. Donnelley & Sons Company, Harrisonburg, Virginia

1 3 5 7 9 10 8 6 4 2

FOR ASA STAHL

Bongo Fishing: n. **1.** To go on an adventurous trip somewhere at least ten light years away. **2.** To set off on any unusual expedition, not knowing what its outcome will be. **3.** Non-invasive fishing for the colorful bongo fish in the Pleiades. **4.** Slang: *"Let's bongo down to Orion, man."*

—*Zecster's Intergalactic Dictionary* (14th Pleiades edition)

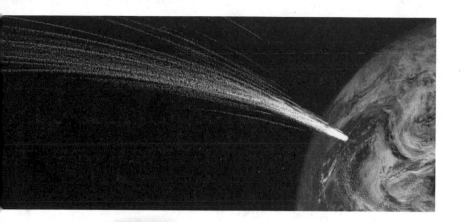

One

Something far out in space, maybe even beyond Mars, was hurtling toward Earth. It was metallic, about the size of a car, and going very fast. It was going so fast that it would be hard to see what it was, or what was inside it, yet it seemed to know exactly where it was going. It was going so fast that a regular spaceship traveling at 17,000 miles an hour would have looked like it was standing still as our small metallic object passed it, and the astronauts inside would have seen only a streak that vanished almost as soon as it appeared. No telescope would have seen it, no normal earth radar, though there were many people on Earth, both good and bad, who would have liked to see it. Smoke trailed behind the metallic object, lights blinked on and off inside, and it exuded a general air of efficiency and well-worn experience as it barreled along at super-hypersonic speed.

On Earth, it was the end of the school day. Jason Jameson sat in class daydreaming while Ms. Rothbar talked about poetry and her pet poodle. Jason was drawing a doodle of a really fast car on his math homework while Ms. Rothbar talked, and he was wondering when the bell would ring. Then he wondered what he would do when he got home, and then he wondered why it seemed like nothing was going on in his life.

Just a cloudy day in Berkeley, fog coming across the bay, seagulls whirling above the soccer field outside.

Out in space, the bright metallic object (was it green?) drew closer to Earth, and if you had been inside looking out, you would have seen Earth like a huge green-and-blue ball hanging in front of you, oceans and deserts and cities spread over its perfect curve.

The metallic object began, finally, to slow. It veered a little to the left and then made a turn and pointed straight down toward the eastern edge of the Pacific Ocean, foggy where the cold water met the warm land. The metallic object tried to find a clear landing place, but now something seemed awry, and it shivered and shook and refused to change course. Down it went, closer to the fog bank. It wobbled and shuddered and sped on.

At last the bell rang. Jason gathered his books and stuffed them in his backpack and started off for home, down Ninth Street, then left on Harrison. He was lost in thought, but later he wouldn't be able to remember anything about what he had been thinking. His feet pattered down the street, and he counted in time to his footsteps, trying not to step on the cracks, enjoying the rhythm of his walking.

He heard a sound above him, small and far away, different from other city sounds.

Far away at first and then a little closer: in the air somewhere, in the low clouds. Jason turned to look up as the sound grew louder, but there was nothing to see. A black car with shiny hubcaps rolled down the street, stereo rattling its windows, turned the corner, and disappeared.

The sound from above grew louder and louder, until it became a screeching yowl that hurt Jason's eardrums. He stood like a statue with his mouth open, staring up. Out of the clouds the metallic object appeared, close now and going very fast.

It was heading straight toward him.

Jason froze. Everything seemed to be happening in slow motion. His heart was racing, there was no time to

think or even move the tiniest bit. Louder and louder, closer and closer the object came at him.

Then—

Silence.

The object stopped dead in the air, a dark shape looming just above Jason. He heard a small hissing sound, like steam escaping from a valve, and the clank of metal on metal. The object hesitated for a moment and then veered off, careening into the empty industrial lot next to him. *WHUMP*—it landed in the far corner of the lot, behind a pile of dirt. A cloud of smoke and dust billowed up.

Jason doubled over with relief, inhaling big gulps of air. He steadied himself against a telephone pole. His legs shook, his hands were sweaty, his heart rattled in his chest. What could it have been? A satellite? A bomb? A plane crash? How could it have stopped in midair? His heart still pounding, he stood up and looked across the empty lot. Clouds of steam curled up from behind the pile of dirt.

A big truck drove down the street but rumbled past without stopping. Everything seemed just as before, except for the steam hissing from the empty lot. Jason, still leaning against the telephone pole, wondered whether the police were coming. Shouldn't they be screeching around the corner to deal with this emergency? But there was nothing, just the same gray afternoon sky, the same fog whispering in, the same empty Ninth Street.

No one had seen the strange object except Jason. How could that be? Should he run for help? Call the police? He looked more intently at the pile of dirt and the steam rising up. He wanted to take a peek, but something held him back. Maybe it was a bomb about to blow up?

Then he thought, I could look at it for just a second. Just to check it out. His legs still shaking, he made his way across the lot and scrambled to the top of the pile of dirt.

Smoke billowed up in front of him, and he squinted, trying to see through it. The hissing seemed to be quieting down, and he heard a sound like a hubcap falling to the ground. Something seemed to draw him in, and he crept closer. He heard a groan, then muttering in a language he didn't understand: *"Beedleupgogborpzzzt zzzt krum!"* Then loud, hacking coughs.

The voice started again, but this time in English: "Crummy no-good dust drive. Knew I shoulda fixed it before I left!"

Jason stood transfixed, peering through the smoke. Out of the haze, reaching through something like a car window, appeared a small, slightly blue hand.

Jason recoiled from the hand, but then he was fascinated and moved nearer. When he was a few feet away, the voice called out, "Isn't this Earth?"

"Yyyes, this is Earth."

"How about a hand? Door's busted shut." More hacking coughs and the sound of a car door rattling. The hand beckoned to him, and the voice said, "Don't worry, just do it."

Jason reached out to touch the hand and felt a shock, almost electric. It grabbed tightly onto his hand, and, surprised, he pulled away. As he did, he fell over backward and landed in the dirt. Whatever he was holding went flying over his head. Jason lay on the ground for a moment, then sat up and turned around.

A small man stood in front of him, alternately coughing and energetically dusting off his clothes. He was about the same height as Jason, but much older, old enough to be a grandfather. He had silvery white hair, a black baseball cap, faded blue jeans, and a jacket that reminded Jason of something a race-car driver would wear. On his feet was a pair of purple high-top sneakers.

Jason studied the man's face. He had bright eyes that seemed amused by what they saw around him, and a crooked nose. His face, like his hands, was slightly blue. The man looked up from cleaning his jacket and broke into a laugh.

"Whatcha lookin' at, kid?" he said, then went on brushing himself off. He picked a piece of straw out of his hair, flicked it away, and reached into his jacket pocket to pull out a card, which he held out to Jason. "The name's Sam. Samuel X. Orbit."

Jason looked down at the card. It looked like an ordinary business card, but a little more mysterious.

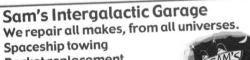

Sam's Intergalactic Garage
We repair all makes, from all universes.
Spaceship towing
Rocket replacement
Hot rod rockets

Samuel X. Orbit, prop.
No job too small, no galaxy too far.
Phone: 1(426) 800-34587697-2000467582
12765 Interstellar Road, Pleiades 20567

The man bowed low with an exaggerated swing of his arm. "Glad to meet you, kid." He held out his hand for Jason to shake.

Jason stared. Where had he come from? What was he doing here? Was he really from outer space? Was he an alien? Was this a joke? A trick played by someone from

Telegraph Avenue? Jason felt nervous. What was he supposed to say to an alien who had landed in Berkeley, whose smoking spaceship was sitting in an empty lot on Ninth Street? What if he wasn't an alien at all, but some weirdo from San Francisco? It seemed like he had come in from that direction.

Jason's mind was racing, and his mother's words rang in his ears: "Don't talk to strangers!"

This was definitely a stranger.

He tried to think of something to say, but nothing would come out of the rush of his thoughts. Standing at attention, he blurted, "Alien! I come in peace!" in a high, scared-sounding voice.

The small man burst out laughing, his eyes twinkling. The more he thought about what Jason had said, the funnier it seemed to him, until he was doubled over in laughter. He regained his composure and said, "Hey, kid, that's my line. *I* come in peace. *You* live here."

Jason was taken aback by this response. He relaxed his shoulders and stared at the little man. Whatever he was, he seemed very comfortable on Earth. Jason felt reassured. At least this being who called himself Sam could talk to people on Earth.

"What's your name, kid?"

"Jason. Jason Jameson."

"Jason, hmmmm? I knew a Jason on Orion 26 one

time. Gave me a lift for a couple of light-years when this blasted machine conked out on me."

"Orion? Is that out past Concord somewhere? Out in the suburbs?"

"Yeah," Sam said, "way past Concord. About 1,344 light-years past Concord, give or take a few parsecs here and there, and not counting if one wants to take a detour to the Pleiades, which is where I live. That's only 410 light-years away. Ever been there, kid?" Sam's eyes sparkled.

Ever been there? This was getting out of hand. "Uh, no, not recently."

"Not recently?" Sam said. "You mean like, never?"

"I haven't even been to New York."

"Well, anyway," Sam said. "So you're probably wondering what I'm doing in this empty lot in Berkeley, California. This is Berkeley, isn't it?"

"Yes," said Jason.

"Thought so. At least that's what the Omni-Locator said. By the way, thanks for pulling me out. And sorry about the close call back on the street there. Steering's a little loose." Sam pulled a piece of grass out of his ear. "Took the Dart out for a spin to test the new turbo drive I put in. Slipped it into thirty-sixth gear out near Pluto, thinking I'd slingshot around the sun and then home to the Pleiades, when it conked out on me. There I am out in the middle of the asteroids with no power. Then

I think, Earth! It's only a few million miles away, so I zip over here and manage the reentry angle, but then the steering gets a little funny on me and I have to make an emergency landing in your fair city. Wouldn't you know it? Just when Edna had a delicious dinner cooking."

"Edna? Who's Edna? Is she in the spaceship with you?"

"Cooking in the spaceship? No way. Can't fit a stove in my spaceship. She's my wife, back home in the Pleiades, making a ruckus in the kitchen and cooking up something scrumptious."

"Oh." Jason liked the way this alien talked. There was something comfortable about him, even if his skin was slightly blue. Sam reminded him of his uncle Miltie in Los Angeles. Uncle Miltie was an auto mechanic, too.

"Any good at fixing stuff?" Sam was looking intently at Jason. "Like broken-down spaceships?"

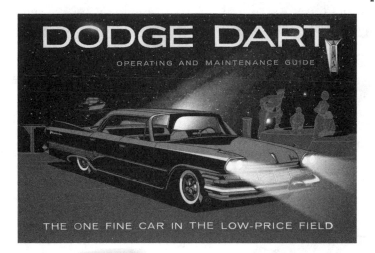

TWO

DODGE DART

OPERATING AND MAINTENANCE GUIDE

THE ONE FINE CAR IN THE LOW-PRICE FIELD

am and Jason turned and stood side by side, looking through the last wisps of smoke that curled up from the hissing object. Sam waved his arms to get rid of the smoke.

"What d'ya think?"

In front of them was something that looked strangely like a dented, slightly rusty, and well-singed lime-green 1960 Dodge Dart, except smaller.

"That's a spaceship?"

Sam smiled. "Of course! What did you think it might be? A bulldozer? I mean, well, it is an older-model ship.

I haven't put in the new dark-energy turbo drive like the latest models. Rides a little rougher than the new ones, especially at the slower gears like two times light speed." Sam took off his cap and ran his fingers through his hair, looking lovingly at the car. "A real peach for interstellar travel. Does about ten light-years a minute if it's tuned up. Comfortable, too. Look at those red leather seats."

"It looks like a Dodge Dart," said Jason, who knew a lot about cars. He liked to look at old books and magazines about cars. His favorite car was a Porsche Speedster.

"Yeah, what of it?" Sam said, looking sideways at him.

"Aren't spaceships shaped like saucers, round and shiny and bright, with little windows all around?"

"Those were the old-style ships. History. Those flying-saucer UFOs were so uncomfortable. Hated them. Cramped, no legroom, drove terribly. Scrunchy little portholes. Eccch. Could hardly see a thing when you were flying. Always running into stuff. You call them UFOs; we call them UN-FUN ORDEALs or sometimes GMOHs, as in GET ME OUT OF HEREs."

"Why a Dodge Dart?" Jason thought a Ferrari or a Porsche would make a cooler spaceship. Dodge Darts weren't the greatest-looking cars.

"Something about the aerodynamics and the tail fins makes them right for galaxy hopping. The scientist guys from the next galaxy searched all over the cosmos for the right car, and—bingo!—they came up with a 1960 Dodge Dart as the perfect spaceship, top of the line for intergalactic travel. Of course, they had to sneak the Dart plans away from Earth without you Earthlings finding out about it. Funny the way humans are so worried about people from other places coming to visit. Every time a couple of tourists drop in from the Andromeda Galaxy to see the Grand Canyon or the Empire State Building, everyone gets all upset and thinks it's some kind of invasion or something. Never could understand that.

"Anyway, they had to fiddle with the plans quite a bit, and of course the old slant-six engine is gone; you need something a little more powerful to get across the galaxy. Otherwise it's pretty much a top-of-the-line 1960 Dodge Dart Phoenix. Still has that push-button TorqueFlite Six transmission and super-tight vacuum-lock windows. Great views out the windows, too. Lots of visibility."

Jason looked at the car. It did seem to have big windows and lots of room inside.

Sam stood proudly next to it. "Mine has these comfy seats, big stereo, plenty of power. Tinted rear windows, too. They make A-plus ships. Except when they're a little old and tend to conk out in the middle of nowhere, like this one."

Jason looked at Sam and then at the Dart. A blue alien in a Dodge Dart spaceship?

"Here, give me a hand," said Sam. "Let's open up the hood and see what the damage looks like."

Jason warily approached the car.

"It's okay, kid—it won't bite. Put your hands here."

Together they yanked on the hood of the Dart. It creaked loudly but stayed shut.

Sam stood back and scratched his head. "Must've gotten jammed in that landing. Let's try again."

Together . . .

"GRUNTUMPHHH!"

They yanked.

The car rocked, but the hood stayed shut.

Their faces scrunched up, they tried again. *Crack*— the hood flew open, sending them flying backward. Sam picked himself up and brushed the dust off once again.

"Stuck pretty good." He held out his hand to help Jason up.

"Yeah."

They looked under the hood of the Dart.

It didn't look like the engine of any car Jason had ever seen: no carburetor, no radiator, no alternator, and no place for windshield-wiper fluid. He knew what the engine of a car should look like from studying pictures in car magazines. He liked to collect car magazines, and he had been to his uncle Miltie's garage in Los Angeles and seen him fixing all kinds of engines.

Instead of what Jason expected, there was a tangle of

wires and tubes that glowed, sparked, and turned bright fluorescent colors. Some were like tiny strings of stars; others, tubes of glowing water circling around and around. The tubes came out of bright chrome spheres and went back into other spheres; strings of stars wound around tanks of strange liquids. Miniature gears seemed to be made of clear plastic, and Jason could see through them into the heart of the engine itself. Below the tubes, in the middle of the tangle of lights, there was a bubbling tank of what looked like orange Gatorade.

"Like I said, dust drive's on the fritz." Sam rubbed his chin. "Not good. This could take a while to fix."

"Dust drive? What's that?"

"Like a generator, except it runs on dust."

"Dust? Like lint or something?"

"Oh, no, not that kind. It collects intergalactic dust when you're traveling through space and converts it into energy. Makes the regular fuel last longer, kind of like with your hybrid cars. It's got all the dust it needs, but the bearings need a special kind of lubricant, and I forgot to bring some. Dang. Edna's not gonna be too happy if I'm late for dinner."

"Late for dinner?"

"It'll take me at least an hour to get home to our planet in the Pleiades. Two hours if the traffic's bad. That's presuming I can get this thing up and running somehow. My wife hates it if dinner gets cold."

"But you said you live 410 light-years away." Jason knew that a light-year was a long, long distance. Like trillions of miles. Or maybe zillions.

"What of it?" Sam looked intently at the boy and squinted his eyes with a quizzical expression. Then a light seemed to dawn, and he smiled brightly. "Oh, yeah, right, I forgot."

"Forgot?"

"I forgot that here on Earth you can design something as beautiful as a Dodge Dart, but you haven't learned to put the pedal to the metal yet—you know, go reaaaaalllllly fast." Sam drew the word out as long as he could.

"The space shuttle goes seventeen thousand miles an hour," said Jason. "That's pretty fast."

"Chicken feed," said Sam, "chicken feed. I mean, that's like a tiny fraction of the speed of light. Drop in the bucket. Here, I'll show you how it works."

He knelt on the ground and began to draw with a stick in the dirt. It looked like a diagram or a map, but not like any map Jason had seen before. Sam talked while he drew, stopping occasionally to point with his stick at the complicated drawing.

"Two guys on Orion named Zorgle and Borgle figured out that if you get down to the level of quarks, which is way smaller than atoms, all sorts of interesting stuff starts to happen, like EPR correlations and entangled particles.

"Then if you take the coefficient of the inverse ratio of the subzero general mass of the ionic plasma and divide it by the optimum transverse inducer ratio, you get something called a . . . uh . . . what's it called?" He stopped and scratched his head. "Sleepy cat reaction, or something like that. Or was it a dog-bone inversion? The level shift in the quark plasma field can make solid objects slip through space without much friction. Then you can go fast, really fast. Fast as a greased frog in chicken fat."

Jason smiled.

"Got it so far, kid?"

"I think so. I mean, sort of." But he didn't. Not at all. This was way beyond anything Ms. Rothbar had taught their class.

Sam started in again. "So, out in the galaxy there's these things called cosmic wormholes, but they're not wormholes in wood, they're big tunnels out in space, and they make it real easy to get around. We use ionic plasma generators, which come with their antigravity regulators installed, and that takes care of the coefficient subparticle repulsion rollers. . . ."

Sam was talking fast, engrossed in what he was saying, and Jason's mind began to wander. He looked down at the drawing in the dirt, which was getting more and more difficult to understand. Then he heard something about marshmallows and energy somethings and gerbils.

Sam stood up. "Anyway, Zorgle and Borgle were the ones who figured it out. Changed the universe forever. Meant we could go much faster than the speed of light. Don't know why you folks on Earth haven't caught up yet. Sometimes I wonder if you like to go slow."

"We only learned to fly a hundred years ago." Jason felt as if he had to defend his planet's reputation.

"Right, I forgot. A young civilization. Earthlings will get the hang of it eventually. Then you won't be scared bunnies: 'We can't fly faster than light—we're so afraid terrible things might happen.'"

Jason tried to smile as if he understood everything Sam had said, but of course he didn't. Science with Ms. Rothbar didn't go much beyond the basics. He was never quite sure if she understood what she was teaching anyway. She seemed to know a lot about animals and fairy tales and knitting, but not science.

"Gee, I don't know . . . ," said Jason, his voice trailing off. "I mean, cars can't fly, no matter how fast they can go. They don't have wings." He thought about the movie *E.T.*, and the scene at the end where the kids flew on bikes. That didn't seem very real. He also remembered a children's book with pictures of a flying blue Cadillac. That was the kind of thing that happened only in stories.

"Yeah, of course," Sam said, "cars can't fly. How many cars do you see flying down the street around here?

Truth is, what a car needs for flying you ain't got here on Earth. Everywhere else in the universe you can see cars waltzing across the sky, but you poor Earthlings are still poking along on highways, stuck in traffic jams."

Jason looked quizzically at Sam.

"It's pretty simple, actually. You need gravity rotators. They amplify gravity fields and then reverse them. Send them back where they came from, or somewhere like that. They make the car float because they make their own antigravity field."

Sam turned and pointed down inside the engine compartment of the Dart. On either side of the engine were two red boxes with big switches on the side. A metal plate was attached to each.

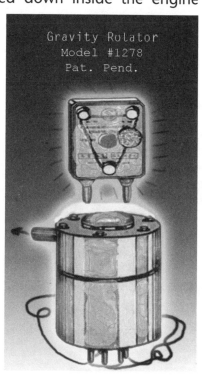

Gravity Rotator
Model #1278
Pat. Pend.

"When you land, they deactivate automatically. When you take off, they switch on."

"Hmmm," said Jason. The more Sam talked, the less it made sense.

"Don't worry, you'll understand it eventually. You look like a smart kid," Sam said, reaching for some wires that trailed off the engine. He gave a sharp tug and suddenly jumped back, as if he had gotten a shock. "Dang, I thought that was grounded. This thing's losing its marshmallows."

Three

*S*am muttered to himself as he worked on the engine, adjusting bolts and tying bits of string together. After a while, with his head deep in the engine compartment, he called out, "Isn't there a deli around the corner?"

"Yeah—but how did you know—"

"I'm starving. That scrumptious dinner of Edna's will have to wait. I need to eat NOW." He pulled himself up and wiped his hands off with a grease rag. "I remember that deli from last time I was here."

"You've been here before?"

"Oh, sure, we like to drop in. Earth is one of our favorite places in the universe. Great pastrami sandwiches at that deli, yes? And I think they've got something that can fix the drive."

Jason looked at Sam. Aliens who liked to visit Earth and eat pastrami sandwiches?

"What d'ya say, kid, how about a bite to eat?"

"Oh, I should be getting home," said Jason, not meaning it at all.

"Is your mom waiting for you?"

"No, she doesn't get home till later."

"What time does your dad come home?"

"He's gone."

"Gone? You mean, like, left?"

"No, he died a few years ago."

"I'm sorry to hear it, kid. That must be tough."

"Yeah, sometimes." Jason thought of his father. He had a few memories of him, but it was hard to grasp on to anything concrete about a person who had only been in his life for such a short time. An emptiness in the back closet of his mind.

"Any brothers or sisters?"

"No."

"Well, that's no fun," Sam said.

Jason nodded and looked at the ground. He didn't mind being an only child, but he hated it when people took pity on him for it.

"So. Your mom's not home and you've got nothing

to do but go home and watch TV, and you won't spend some time keeping a visitor from another planet company, friendly-like?"

"I guess I could," said Jason.

Sam smiled at him as he put away his grease rag. They covered up the Dart with some branches from the back of the lot, and then walked out from behind the dirt piles and onto Ninth Street. Turning left on Gilman, they headed up toward the deli on San Pablo. Jason wondered if anyone would notice Sam's blueness, but then he thought that he wasn't that blue, and if you weren't looking too closely, you might not notice it at all. Then again, he was kind of a small, odd-looking person.

Luckily, the passersby were wrapped up in their own thoughts and didn't seem to notice Sam. There were always odd-looking people walking the streets of Berkeley.

And no one looked up as Sam and Jason walked into the deli. Jason decided that if anyone asked about this strange person with him, he would say that his friend Sam was a midget with the circus and he suffered from a rare heart disease, which caused a certain amount of blueness in his skin, and thank you very much for being a little more considerate with someone who suffered from such a rare and incurable disease.

They sat at a table near the front and split a pastrami sandwich. Sam bit into his half with enthusiasm, chomping loudly and occasionally burping.

Halfway through the sandwich, and out of the corner of his mouth, which was full of food, Sam said, "Hab you god a poget to put some kedgup in?"

"Kedgup? What's that?"

Gulping the rest of his sandwich down, Sam whispered, "You know, ketchup." Reaching out, he grabbed a fistful of ketchup packages from the rack on the table.

"Gee, that's a lot of ketchup."

"It's for the Dart. Works as good as axle grease, and it's a lot cheaper. Also Edna likes to save the little packages for barbecues."

As they walked out, Sam reached over the next table and grabbed all those ketchup packages, too. He motioned to Jason to grab the ketchup from the next table. Jason stuffed the ketchup down into his sweatshirt, looking around to make sure no one was watching.

Outside, Sam adjusted his cap and smiled. "Can never have enough ketchup. Or marshmallows."

Four

"Marshmallows?" asked Jason. "For the engine?"

"Uh, yeah, sort of, uh, most of them anyway. A big bag, if we can find one. How about in there?" Sam pointed at the grocery store on the corner of Gilman and San Pablo.

"Okay," said Jason, "I'll see how much money I have left." While Sam waited outside, he went in and picked out the biggest bag of marshmallows he could afford.

Back at the spaceship, they cleared away the

branches and Sam opened the hood. Slowly, one by one, he squeezed the ketchup from the packages down into a kind of plastic bottle at the back of the engine.

"Got the marshmallows?" asked Sam.

Jason handed him the bag.

"Watch." Sam opened the bag and threw one of the marshmallows high in the air. He tilted his head back and opened his mouth wide, deftly catching the marshmallow in his mouth. He did this with three marshmallows in a row and then happily chewed all three of them together, smiling at Jason and looking like a hamster.

"Mmmm, dewicious. Want one?" Still chewing loudly, Sam held the package out for Jason.

Jason threw a marshmallow in the air, tilting his head back like Sam, but the marshmallow bounced off his nose and into the dirt.

"Don't worry, you'll get the hang of it. Took me forty-four bags."

Sam turned his attention back to the car. He stuffed several of the marshmallows down one of the glowing tubes, put the cap back on, fiddled with one of the bright wires, then slammed the hood of the Dart shut.

"That should do it. Now the door."

He pulled a small purple wrench out of his pocket and worked on the broken door, swinging it back and forth and slamming it until it stopped squeaking. Then he climbed into the Dart, carefully putting the bag of marshmallows next to him on the seat.

"Time to go." He smiled up at Jason, who stood with his hand on the car, looking through the window.

Jason watched, fascinated, as Sam began quickly pulling levers and pushing buttons on the dashboard and the ceiling above him, looking like an airline pilot Jason had seen in a movie, getting ready for takeoff. Some buttons seemed to wiggle and vibrate as he pulled them, and others glowed with a strange purple light. Still others flashed on and off in circles and curlicues.

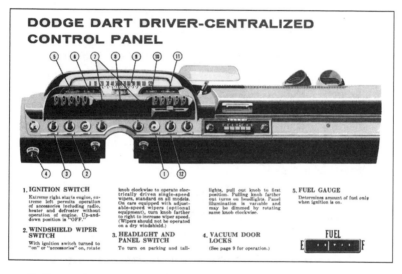

DODGE DART DRIVER-CENTRALIZED CONTROL PANEL

1. **IGNITION SWITCH**
Extreme right starts engine, extreme left permits operation of accessories including radio, heater and defroster without operation of engine. Up-and-down position is "OFF."

2. **WINDSHIELD WIPER SWITCH**
With ignition switch turned to "on" or "accessories" on, rotate knob clockwise to operate electrically driven single-speed wipers, standard on all models. On cars equipped with adjustable-speed wipers (optional equipment), turn knob farther to right to increase wiper speed. (Wipers should not be operated on a dry windshield.)

3. **HEADLIGHT AND PANEL SWITCH**
To turn on parking and tail-lights, pull out knob to first position. Pulling knob farther out turns on headlights. Panel illumination is variable and may be dimmed by rotating same knob clockwise.

4. **VACUUM DOOR LOCKS**
(See page 9 for operation.)

5. **FUEL GAUGE**
Determines amount of fuel only when ignition is on.

FUEL
E | | | ▼ | | F

"All set," said Sam. Carefully he pointed a blue finger at a bull's-eye on the dashboard. He sighted down the finger and said, "SHABLAM!"

With a low rumble the car started up.

He grinned out the window at Jason. "A little more dramatic with that *shablam* in there."

The Dart hummed with energy. Glowing red exhaust

pipes shot out hot rocket gases. Sam leaned out the window and shook Jason's hand. "So long, kiddo. Thanks for all the help."

Jason looked at the car. It was fascinating and mysterious and exotic, rumbling quietly as it readied for takeoff. Suddenly he blurted out, "Can I go for a ride?"

"Sorry, kid. Maybe some other time. I'm late already."

The Dart rose off the ground, humming. Jason stood back as it slowly lifted up. He could feel the thrum of its engines in his chest. It climbed steadily into the air, until it was just above the telephone wires.

Sam leaned out the window and called down, "Thanks again! Hey, want to go bongo fishing sometime?"

"Bongo fishing?" That sounded mysterious and fascinating.

"Yeah, bongo—"

As Sam said the words, the Dart accelerated to a tremendous speed and vanished into the sky.

Jason stood for a long time looking up. Then he turned around and started for home. As he walked across the empty lot, he saw a homeless man pushing his shopping cart along Ninth Street, staring up at the sky with his mouth wide open. Jason turned away and headed for home, his mind a jumble of thoughts. Would this alien actually come back? Would he get a chance to ride in the Dodge Dart spaceship? What if he had imagined the whole thing?

Five

Jason looked up as he came to his apartment building. In the front window of their second-floor apartment was Sputnik, the cat, waiting for him to come home from school. Jason walked up the stairs, opened the apartment door, and turned on the lights. He stood in the front hall, listening. The silence enveloped him as he stood, trying to understand what had happened.

Could it be real? Maybe something he ate at lunch had given him delusions. Maybe some weirdo had played a trick on him. Maybe, worst of all possibilities, he was going crazy.

Sputnik pattered up to him and rubbed up against his leg. Good old Sputnik. Sputnik the Wonder Cat, able to leap over tall wastebaskets, chase his tail for two hours, pee in the toilet, sometimes even wink and twist his nose at the same time. Then again, he was also a kind of hypochondriac, always sick with something, always going to the vet.

Jason reached down to pet him. "Good Sputs, that's a good cat."

He looked around. The couch was still in the living room, the TV in the corner by the window, his mother's faded Beatles poster on the wall. As he went around turning on lights in the apartment, everything seemed cozy and reassuring. Even the bedspread that his mom had put over the couch to cover the frayed upholstery seemed like an old friend.

In the kitchen he found the last two chocolate chip cookies at the bottom of the box, then he went back to the living room and turned on the TV. He sat on the couch, munching the cookies and switching from channel to channel.

Maybe there would be something on the news about a visitor from outer space. Maybe the authorities already knew about the Dodge Dart spaceship and had everything figured out. But none of the TV shows talked about a flying Dart or a small alien with blue skin named Sam.

Jason searched in his pockets for the card Sam had given him, but it had disappeared. Maybe he had dropped it as the spaceship took off or left it at the deli. Maybe there *was* no card.

The card had said "Sam's Intergalactic Garage." What did that mean? What was an intergalactic garage? Robots fixing shiny spaceships? Or Sam in an old building, keeping Darts together with ketchup?

Should he tell his mom? She would probably think he was crazy. He did have a reputation for being a space cadet.

Maybe he should tell it all to Sputnik, to see how it sounded. What good would that do? He was a cat. Then again, sometimes Sputnik seemed like his best friend. Jason had named him after the Russian satellite that was the first to orbit the Earth; when Sputnik was a kitten, he always seemed to be trying to launch himself into space by jumping off the furniture, and once he even jumped off the second-floor stairs.

Maybe telling the story to Sputnik would be good practice. Jason sat down on the floor in front of the cat and started in, sticking strictly to the facts and leaving out no details. As he got to the exciting part about the red-hot car flying out of the sky, Sputnik yawned and walked into the kitchen.

Soon, Jason's mother, Ann, came home. "Hi, honey," she called out, hanging up her coat. Then she came into the living room and sat down next to Jason.

"Anything terrific on TV?"

That was his mother's way of saying that she thought everything on TV was a waste of time.

When it was time for dinner, Jason sat daydreaming as he ate his chicken and mashed potatoes. Sputnik was draped sideways over his lap, his front legs hanging down on one side, rear legs on the other, purring contentedly. Sam and his wife, Edna—what did they eat for dinner? Did they eat bongo fish? Could a Dodge Dart really fly across the universe? The Dart was so much more interesting than his mom's Ford Taurus. A Taurus would never fly, that was for sure. . . .

His mother's voice brought him back: "Jason, watch out! You're spilling the potatoes."

He looked down. The mashed potatoes were on Sputnik's head. Poor Sputnik. Stuff was always happening to him. Once a truck had almost run him over, and another time he had swallowed a rubber ball and had to go to the vet. Then he had gotten lost for a week, and Jason's mom went to a pet psychic to find out where he was. The psychic went into a trance and said that a man in a red sports car had taken Sputnik to his house in the hills and was feeding him fancy cat food. But then, a week later, they found Sputnik under Mrs. Sherbatskoy's house next door, trapped in the crawl space, half starved. Jason's mother complained to the pet psychic, but she gave them back only half their money, saying that perhaps the man had brought Sputnik back, and *then* he got stuck under Mrs. Sherbatskoy's.

In bed that night, Jason pored over *The Giant Atlas of the Universe for Boys and Girls*, which his uncle Miltie had bought for him at Christmas the year before. Did stars have numbers? Did galaxies have numbers? What was the name of that galaxy Sam talked about, that started with an *A*, the one the alien tourists came from? In the index Jason found it: the Andromeda Galaxy. It was described as "part of the Local Group." (What did that mean?) The book said that "there are about 35 galaxies in the Local Group, which is dominated by our own Milky Way and two other large spiral galaxies—the Andromeda Galaxy and the Pinwheel Galaxy. The Andromeda Galaxy is 2.5 million light-years away."

Jason turned out the light and lay back in bed looking up through his window. The city lights were bright and he could see only a few stars in the night sky, but he gazed at them, wondering if one of the stars was where Sam lived. Then he thought, That's impossible. I imagined it all. Nobody lives out there. It's only white-hot stars and bits of rock floating through space.

But somehow it didn't seem as if he'd imagined it.

And somewhere not too far away, in the still of the night, in the basement of an old house with a strange antenna on top, someone else was thinking about UFOs and aliens and faraway galaxies. In his garage was a small black car, which also had a funny, round antenna on top.

He sat crouched in front of a computer, his face lit by the glow of the screen as he gnawed at a chocolate chip cookie and crumbs littered his beard. He roamed across the internet, muttering to himself, probing and poking into places he shouldn't, studying things from very, very far away; where they came from and where they might be going, where they might land, where they might crash. Though this person was part of a well-known profession, and a generally upstanding member of his community, his life revolved around a plan to steal something from very, very far away and make it his own. No one knew of this plan. He had to keep it secret, for he had tried once before to steal something from the farthest reaches of the galaxy. He had just missed getting caught, and knew that if he made one wrong move, all his efforts would come to naught. But still he looked and searched and struggled to find what he wanted.

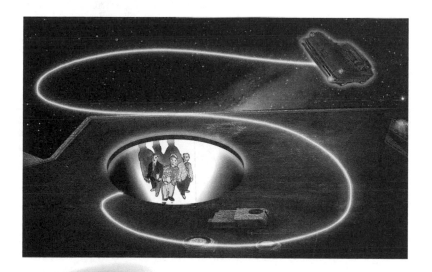

Six

*T*he next day after school, Jason decided to go to the library and do some investigating.

He found a car magazine from 1960, which had an article about the Dodge Dart. He discovered that 1960 was the first year that Dodge Darts were made, and that everyone thought they were pretty good cars when they came out. "The Dart: An Entirely New American Automobile!" was the headline. It talked about what a powerful engine the Dart had, how it could "whip the froth off the head of a beer," and how it was "effortless to drive." It also said that the Dart "employs Unibody construction and is vat-dipped in a series of pickling solutions to stave off rust and corrosion." Sam's Dart certainly hadn't staved off rust and corrosion. At the end of the article there was a little note that said "See *Automotive Mystery World*, May 1960, for an interesting story about the introduction of the Dart."

"Do you happen to have the May 1960 issue of *Automotive Mystery World*?" he asked the librarian.

She looked on her computer. "No, I'm sorry, that's no longer listed. It must have been thrown out. It was only published for a short while."

"Rats."

"Then again," said the librarian, "sometimes things don't get thrown out. Librarians never like to throw things away. Maybe it's still in the storeroom." She disappeared through a door that said EMPLOYEES ONLY. Soon she came back with an old cardboard box and set it on the counter.

"Maybe," she said, shrugging her shoulders.

Jason carried the box to a table and pulled out the magazines one by one. At the bottom, there was the May 1960 issue of *Automotive Mystery World*. He fished it out and blew the dust off. People in the reference room coughed. Jason opened the yellowing magazine and found that, sure enough, on page 72, there was a short article by Hank Sniffle. It said that in 1959, when the designers of the Dart were working on the plans and had built two full-scale models of the car, one of them disappeared out of the factory design department during the night, along with a full set of plans for the engine and the construction of the car. At first the rival Ford Motor Company was suspected of the theft, but they were later found to be innocent of any wrongdoing, and the mystery had never been solved. The plans had seemingly vanished into thin air. The only clue was a large, perfectly round hole that was burned through the ceiling of the auto design department, a hole exactly big enough to lift a Dodge Dart through. Jason's eyes grew wide. He left the library feeling even odder than the day before.

All that week, Jason could think of nothing but Sam and the Dart. More than once his mother had to call him out of his daydreams, saying, "Earth to Jason, Earth to Jason" and "Where you been, stranger?" He dreamt about Sam, and thought about him while he was eating his cereal and while he was trying to concentrate in school. One day he thought that it was all his imagination, and the next he was sure it had really happened.

"I'm going to a yoga workshop on Saturday morning," said Jason's mother at breakfast on Thursday. "I'll be back around noon, and you have soccer practice in the afternoon. I called Mrs. Sherbatskoy next door and she said she will be around Saturday morning in case you need anything."

Saturday morning, while Jason was still in bed, she leaned in his room and said, "I left you a tuna sandwich in the fridge in case you get hungry before I get back."

Jason opened one eye and mumbled, "And if I need anything, don't be afraid to knock on Mrs. Sherbatskoy's door."

"Yes, dear," said his mother as she kissed him on the cheek and said good-bye.

He stayed in bed as long as he could, but finally got up and poured a bowl of cereal and milk. He sat watching TV in his pajamas, while slurping his cereal. He was almost finished when he heard the doorbell ring. Who would ring the doorbell at this time on a Saturday morning? It must be somebody wanting a donation, or selling a vacation to Hawaii.

Jason dragged a chair to the front door and peered out the peephole. There was no one there. The doorbell rang again. He stood on his tiptoes and peered down as far as he could through the peephole. When he did that, he could see the top of a small baseball cap.

"Who is it?"

"Who do you think it is?" a familiar voice called back.

Jason opened the door. "Sam!"

This time the little blue man was wearing a purple baseball cap that said INTERGALACTIC ALL-STARS in gold letters. Jason's eyes slowly traveled down Sam: a brown fishing vest, strange fishing tools hanging out of the pockets, a belt with a shiny buckle, and brown pants that looked like they might be waterproof. On his feet, black rubber boots.

"Whatcha lookin' at, kid? Never seen somebody dressed up for a little bongo fishing? I hear they're biting in the south Pleiades, so I thought I'd head up there and try my luck. Want to come along?"

Jason gulped, thinking, What if this alien is here to kidnap me and take me away forever? Or do terrible experiments on me and then leave me in some cornfield in Iowa?

He stared at Sam. "How did you find out where I live?"

"Easy. I Googled you."

Jason looked at Sam in his fishing outfit, with his vest with all the little pockets, and his lures stuck in the brim of his cap, and his bright eyes, and he felt okay. Something in him knew that this fast-talking creature from the Pleiades would be the right person to go with on a fishing trip to outer space. It *was* a long way to go on a Saturday morning before soccer practice, but the idea of traveling in the Dart was too astounding to turn down.

"I have to get dressed and grab a sandwich."

"Don't worry about sandwiches. Edna made some

delicious gollywhoggers. Oh, and by the way, Edna sends her regrets. Says she'd love to meet you, but her bunions are acting up and she doesn't feel like going out."

Jason stopped. "What about my mom? I have to get back by noon."

Sam tipped his cap toward Jason. "Not to worry, kid. Sam and the Dart always get you home on time."

Seven

"Edna also made some glazed doughnuts," said Sam as they walked down the street. "I love glazed doughnuts."

Jason liked glazed doughnuts too.

"The important thing, though, is that she sent along the doughnut holes. Those are for the bongo fish. Bongo fish love glazed doughnut holes."

"Hmmmm," said Jason. "Do bongo fish play the bongos?" He was smiling at Sam.

"Bongos? What are bongos?"

Jason pretended to be playing drums with his hands.

"Haven't seen them play the drums yet, but you never know with bongo fish," said Sam.

"What are gollywhoggers?" asked Jason.

"Delicious, kid."

They came to the empty lot on Ninth Street, and there, behind the piles of dirt, sat the Dart.

"Polished it up a bit since the last trip," Sam said proudly. "Got rid of some of that rust."

The car didn't look much different to Jason, except that attached to the back was a boat trailer, and on the trailer sat a small, dented aluminum rowboat, tightly tied down. In the rowboat was a set of old wooden oars. Jason found himself wondering how a rowboat with oars thrown across the seat could travel across the universe.

"Hop in," Sam said.

The door shut with a solid *thunk*. Jason settled into the big red leather seat and looked at the dashboard. Sam started up the engine. The Dart purred to life, and the dials on the dashboard snapped on. They flickered and jumped, and the engine thrummed with a deep growl.

This is it, thought Jason. His palms felt sticky, and he had a sudden urge to jump out of the Dart and run back home, turn the TV on loud, and forget that Sam had ever existed.

"Nervous?" asked Sam.

"A little."

"Don't worry, the Dart's all fixed up. It'll run like a top. Could you push that button there? The force field covers the boat and keeps the oars from flying out. Cuts down on the rattling when you're above light speed."

The Dart slowly rose off the ground. Jason looked down; a mother was pushing her baby in a stroller. The woman was looking straight ahead, but the baby was looking up at the Dart with eyes wide open, pointing a stubby finger skyward.

Eight

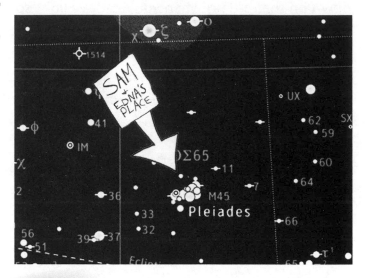

In a minute they were high above the city. Houses and trees glowed far below them in the morning light, and farther away the skyscrapers of Emeryville poked into the sunshine. The Dart sailed east, over the suburbs around Mount Diablo and the farms beyond. Then they climbed higher into the sky. As they sped upward, the sky grew a deeper blue, and soon it was almost black.

Sam flipped a row of switches with a flourish. "Now we get it up to speed. Real speed."

The Dart curved up into the darkness. Sam pushed

hard on the accelerator, and with a roar they jumped ahead. Jason was shoved back in the seat by the force of the acceleration, and his chest felt like someone was pushing hard on it. The oars in the boat rattled for a moment, and then everything was quiet. The clouds and the Earth outside blurred and fell away. The Dart seemed to leap at the chance to speed into space.

The Earth quickly receded until it was just a ball hanging in the sky behind them. They were no longer in the Earth's comforting blue atmosphere, but surrounded by the deep black of space. Jason's mind was spinning. How could anything travel so fast? The Dart seemed to effortlessly move through space, like a fish in the ocean. Was this really happening? Jason was awed by the strange beauty of the world outside the window.

He saw that they were approaching the moon, a little off to the side. How could they have gotten there so quickly? Didn't the astronauts take days to get to the moon?

In the slanting light from the sun Jason saw giant moon craters with their jagged edges amid oceans of dust—waterless, empty, gray. Then they were past the moon, and looking back, Jason could see the farther side, veiled in deep blackness. Behind the moon, the blue dot of the Earth was getting smaller and smaller.

"Could you grab that map in the glove compartment?" Sam's voice brought Jason out of his reverie.

A map? thought Jason. In the middle of outer space? There's nothing in space, nothing for a million miles.

Still, he obediently rummaged through the glove compartment, which seemed to be filled with candy wrappers and old scraps of paper with strange writing on them. From the back he pulled out something that looked like a map and unfolded it on his lap. At the top it said "TOP SECRET: INTERGALACTIC GOVT USE ONLY. DIV. 32567-D REG. 434490."

"Now, let's see—where are we?" Sam looked at the dials on the dashboard. "Okay, looks like about 23056 North and 4726 East, give or take a few."

The map looked complicated to Jason, unlike any map he had seen before. He could see the Earth and the moon and the other planets on it, but it was covered with crisscrossed lines, and little notations that said things like "Door 1028, do not use for Andromeda" or "Gate 752, direct one-way to Leo."

"Weird," said Jason.

"Yeah, hard to read at first. It's got all the doors and gates and commuter lanes from here out to one hundred light-years."

"What are doors and gates?"

"The way to get somewhere fast." Sam swerved the Dart around in an arc to the right, staring intently at the sky in front of the car. He seemed to be lining the car up with something in front of them. "Remember those cosmic wormholes I was telling you about? People

46

started to notice that some spaceships got to where they were going *much* faster than other ships. Years faster." He flipped a glowing switch above him.

"Everybody scratched their heads at first, but then they figured out about wormholes, and pretty soon they made cosmic maps of everywhere. This was a long time ago, like a couple hundred eons or something." Sam adjusted his seat and leaned closer to the windshield. "Once we get the Dart going pretty good, we'll find the wormhole entrance and cruise down to the Pleiades."

"What makes them faster? How come we can't see them from Earth?"

Sam flipped a series of switches on the dashboard: *click click click click.* "Well, you know, you can't see them." He looked sideways at Jason. "I don't completely understand how they were discovered. Something about quarks and strings and interstellar geometry?"

Jason looked down at the map. "It says 'Pleiades Gate 23, direct commuter lane.' Is that near here?"

"Can't take that. You have to have three passengers in the vehicle."

"Oh." He looked at the map again. "What about this? 'Pleiades Door 134, scenic byway.' Is that near here?"

"That one's great. Goes right by a black hole and a couple of fine nebulae." Sam leaned over to look at the map. "Let's see, that's at 23054 North and 4729 East. Must be right over there."

Jason looked, but saw only pinpricks of distant stars ahead of them. "I don't see anything," he said.

"Like I said, you can't see them. Just got to know where they are."

Click click click. More switches, and the car seemed to vibrate more intensely, the dials on the dashboard creeping into the red zone. Sam opened and closed his hands around the steering wheel, hunching over it and peering into the blackness ahead.

"See that?"

"YES," said Jason, gripping the door handle. They were hurtling toward what looked like a ball of rock.

"Asteroid," said Sam. "Just happens to be right next to our gate."

They sped toward the asteroid, Sam muttering to himself, occasionally adjusting a knob on the dashboard.

At the last second, with the asteroid looming, Sam stepped hard on the accelerator and turned the steering wheel slightly to the right. Once more the car leaped ahead. He pushed a button on the sunshade and a brilliant light flashed out from the front of the car. Jason saw an inky void, its edges rippling, open up in front of them.

"Ohhhhh . . . ," he gasped as the Dart dove into the opening.

There was a rushing sound, like a truck in a tunnel, and the car shivered. Now they were in a solid blackness, empty of stars, empty of everything, a huge noth-ingness in the sky.

The Dart drifted through the dark for several minutes and then blasted out into starlight once again, a light much brighter and more radiant than before. The vibration stopped, and inside it was quiet, with only the slight humming sound of the engine.

The Dart was floating now, closer to the stars but somehow going much faster than before. Jason could feel that they were going very fast, but at the same time it seemed as if they were drifting along on a leisurely drive.

"Now we put it on cruise control, sit back, relax, and watch the sights," Sam said, flipping one last switch and mopping his brow with a handkerchief.

Nine

*T*he Dart hummed quietly, a mellow light glowing from the dashboard onto Sam's and Jason's faces. Jason stared out the window, his nose against the glass. He had seen pictures of galaxies and stars in his atlas of the universe, but traveling at light speed through a wormhole was much more than that. No book could begin to give the feeling of this, thought Jason. The Dart seemed like a tiny guppy swimming through an endless black fishbowl filled with shining diamond stars and galaxies. Or like a bug crawling through a field of dew in the early morning. Glowing dust swirled around stars that were being born, galaxies glowed in clouds of shimmering light, whirlpools of dust rotated around and around.

From his cousin's backyard in northern California, far from the city lights, Jason had been amazed by how many stars there were to see on a clear night. But that was nothing compared to what he saw now.

"Never get used to it," said Sam. "Never get used to it. . . ."

"Wow," said Jason. "It's . . . it's . . . it's like it's . . ." It was beyond anything he could put into words.

He glanced down at the dashboard of the Dart.

"Look!" he said, his mouth open. He could see through the car itself, into the engine and then faintly beyond the car. Even a few stars were visible. He could see the working of the engine, all the brightly colored tubes and bottles pumping glowing liquids back and forth. Even the ketchup, bubbling in its little pot. He began to laugh. "Look, Sam, it's the ketch—"

"Right, forgot to tell you. Going fast in a wormhole changes things. Makes 'em kind of see-through or something. Not so scrunched together. The farther apart the atoms are, the faster you can travel."

Jason held up his hand and stared at it. "Couldn't *we* disappear, like, not be there at all?"

"It all hangs together somehow. You have to go a lot faster than this to start seeing through yourself."

Jason was glad they weren't going that fast. Would

he disappear at a zillion miles an hour? He went back to looking out the window.

Far off to the right was a section of the sky that was blank, empty of stars. It seemed like a hole in the universe that was sucking stars toward it, tearing them apart as they fell toward the center, and then churning them into clouds of dust that disappeared into the nothingness at the center.

"It looks like that hole is eating everything," said Jason.

"Black hole," said Sam. "Big one. See that bluish star over there? That's Vega. You can see it easily from Earth. That black hole near it is called Hades. You got to be careful with the Hades black hole. Even the Dart would have a hard time getting out of that one. Don't want to get too close to the horizon of it. We'd be history. No more soccer, no more pastrami sandwiches."

Jason gripped the door handle. Never get out? Where would they go? It looked like the loneliest place in the universe. He turned to Sam. "Are we going to fall into it?"

"Don't worry, we'll keep away from it. There's so much gravity in a black hole, it kind of twists space and time, makes everything slow down and then sucks it in and squishes it into practically nothing. A car would end up the size of a potato chip. Some people say you can get to another universe through a black hole, but I'd never try that."

"Wow," said Jason.

"How about some music?" said Sam. "Intergalactic radio? Eighty-six thousand stations."

Weird space music for sure, thought Jason.

Sam flipped a knob. Music poured out from all around the car: the front, the floor, the roof, the seats. Even the door handles were vibrating. The music filled Jason's body with sound and rhythms. Sam tapped his hands on the steering wheel.

The music sounded vaguely familiar to Jason, not like space music at all. "Isn't this from Earth?"

"Count Basie. A-plus jazz guy," said Sam. "He could swing."

Jason smiled. He had heard of Count Basie. Didn't his mom listen to Count Basie sometimes?

"We pick it up on the interstellar radio system. If you get out in space far enough, you can find radio programs from almost any year."

Jason leaned back in his seat and let the music wash through him as the Dart drifted across the universe. Although he was a trillion miles from home, in a slightly rusty Dodge Dart spaceship, he felt happy. The universe around him was glorious, more beautiful than anything he had ever seen.

An astronomer could only look through the tiny eye-piece of a telescope, but all Jason had to do was look out the windows of the Dart and the beauty of the cosmos was all around. To think that there were beings living all over the galaxy, driving amazing cars back and forth across the universe as easily as going to the supermarket.

The sky grew brighter as the Dart moved through great clouds of glowing gas. "Pleiades straight ahead," said Sam.

A cluster of stars glimmered in front of them, each one surrounded by bright trails of bluish dust.

Sam pointed. "Our place is there, on a planet near that star called Merope, but we're going to my favorite fishing hole, on a planet near the star called Pleione. Okay, we go left at Electra, and then down that dust lane a piece." Sam pointed again as they drew nearer. "See that blue dot? That planet's where we're headed."

He turned the steering wheel and the Dart arced toward the speck of blue, bright against the black background.

As the Dart drew closer to the planet, Jason could see clouds floating above it, and below the clouds, a deep purple-blue ocean.

Sam pushed a button and a shield rose up from under the Dart and locked in position on the front of the car.

"Heat shield. Gets a little hot going into the atmosphere. Hold on to your hat." The Dart shook and rocked from side to side as they plunged into the atmosphere, the heat shield glowing a dull red. Sam gripped the steering wheel tightly as the Dart rocked, but then, as suddenly as it had started, the vibrating stopped, and again it was quiet. The heat shield lowered as Sam flipped a bank of switches over Jason's head. Now they were flying through the clouds that towered above the planet.

The Dart swooped down through one of the clouds and into the open air. Then it banked over the ocean below. The car was on its side, and Jason's nose was pressed to the window.

The Dart leveled out and flew just above the waves, toward a white beach that stretched in either direction as far as the eye could see.

They roared over the beach and then flew inland over a dense jungle, dark leaves waving in a tropical breeze. Jason wondered what kind of animals lived there. He couldn't see through the forest canopy, but there must be strange creatures hidden in its depths, he thought. Perhaps they were creeping things that came out only at night, with long tails and very big claws. What did they eat for dinner? he wondered. And what if he and Sam got stuck and had to spend the night in the jungle?

Ten

A lake appeared below them in the middle of the jungle, a turquoise-blue jewel in the midst of the dark green. Sam angled the car down and with a light touch landed the Dart on the beach that ringed the lake. The car sputtered to a stop at the edge of the water.

"Welcome to Zorcovado Planet Park," said Sam. "A whole planet left wild forever."

Jason looked out the window. "Is it safe to breathe the air?"

"No problem," Sam said. "It's got plenty of oxygen in it."

"Are you sure?"

"Got a book in the glove compartment that lists all the oxygen planets in the universe. Also the best hotels in the galaxy. Every single intergalactic motel. I've been coming here for years, ever since I was a little kid. My dad used to take me fishing here."

Jason wondered what Sam's dad was like. Did he drive a Dodge Dart spaceship, too?

There was a slight rush of air into the car as he opened the door and stepped out onto the beach. Stretching, he felt light-headed. He inhaled the sweet air, filled with the juicy flavor of a jungle. He leaned on the hood of the Dart. Could this all be real? The lake was still, ringed by tropical trees and huge plants with pink flowers as big as basketballs.

"What are those?" Jason asked, pointing to the flowers.

"They're called rumtums or glumbusters or something. Smell pretty good, don't they?"

A shadow crossed the beach. Three great birds, their wings flapping gently, drifted above. They looked like pelicans, but fluorescent-green pelicans, and a little more prehistoric, with long, pointed bills and spiky talons on their feet.

"We call them chompers," said Sam, shielding his

eyes as he looked up. "They've got big appetites." Jason wondered what chompers liked to eat.

Sam pulled a box of fishing tackle out of the trunk. "Time for bongo fishing."

"I was wondering," said Jason, "what bongo fish taste like?"

"Awful. Just awful."

"Awful? Really? Even with a lot of ketchup on them?"

"Terrible." Sam smiled. "But don't worry, we don't eat the bongo fish."

"Then why are we going fishing for them?"

"You'll see."

They unloaded the boat and pushed it into the water. Sam rowed on one side, Jason on the other. Soon they were in the middle of the lake.

"Hope it's not too late," said Sam. "They like to bite real early in the morning."

He showed Jason how to attach doughnut holes to the spinner lures and how to keep the glazed part from falling off.

"There's no hook," said Jason.

"Hook? Oh, I never use a hook. Wouldn't want to hurt the little guys."

No hook? thought Jason. Isn't that the whole point of fishing?

Sam showed Jason how to cast a line, with a doughnut hole attached, out into the water.

They each cast several lines, and with the lines trailing

behind them, they drifted lazily around the lake, munching on the glazed doughnuts and drinking a thermos of hot chocolate. The doughnut holes attached to the lures bobbed up and down as the water lapped peacefully against the boat. Jason stared at the big glumbuster flowers hanging from the trees and soon his head nodded and his eyes closed. Sam's cap slid over his eyes. He snored softly.

Suddenly, *SPLASH!* Jason jumped up. He looked out over the water, but saw nothing. Whatever it was had disappeared back into the water, and the doughnut holes were still bobbing on the surface. He counted them.

"There's one missing!"

"Time for the show to start," said Sam, waking up.

There was another splash, and another doughnut hole disappeared. Ripples churned the water. A shining fish, bright with color, jumped out of the water and splashed back in. Soon another jumped, a little higher, with different colors. Then another and another. All of a sudden, a huge fish, brilliant purple and orange and red, rose out of the water and jumped straight up, higher than Jason thought a fish could jump, higher than the dolphins he had seen at Marine World. Then, as the first fish sank into the water, other fish jumped into the air and twirled and twisted in the sunlight.

Each was a kaleidoscope of color, a light show of glistening brilliance. All along their bodies were little neon lights that flashed the colors of the rainbow.

Two bongo fish jumped together and did a slow-motion dance in the air, a kind of waltz.

"Time for the music," said Sam. He pulled out a battered radio and turned it on. "Doughnut holes get them on that sugar high, then the music sends 'em into orbit."

The radio played music that people danced to a long time ago. "Frank Sinatra," said Sam. "They love it."

As soon as the music started, the lake was alive with leaping bongo fish. They were all around the rowboat, soaring into the air, dancing with each other, wiggling their tail fins as they skittered across the lake like circus acrobats. There were fish of a thousand colors shimmering in the morning light, bright lights flashing down their sides as they played in the air. There were big purple fish with yellow spots that flashed on and off, and some that were deep red with electric blue lines along their sides. Some of them danced in threes, some in fours, and they seemed to smile as they wiggled their fins. The dances became faster and more elaborate as the fish flew over the boat in great arcs and made long lines, putting their fins together in rhythm and arching their backs like a chorus line. Finally they all jumped in the air together and made a great circle in the sky, each holding on to the next one's tail. They sparkled and wriggled for a moment in the air and then crashed back into the lake with an enormous splash.

The lake grew calm. Jason thought the show was

over, but then one more fish leaped out of the water. He was a big fish, and on his back were three smaller fish. The big fish wriggled and the little fish danced on his back, and at the end of their dance, they seemed to take a bow. They were close enough to touch, when the littlest one slipped and crashed into the boat, between Jason's feet. His tiny eyes looked up helplessly, and Jason carefully picked him up and put him back in the water, waving to the little fish as it wriggled away.

The lake was quiet, the sun glinting off its water, the big jungle flowers all around. Jason felt happy. His fingers tingled from holding the tiny fish, and the colors and beauty of the bongo fish dancing seemed to go somewhere deep inside him and fill him with joy. It was all strange and new, and at the same time soothing and beautiful, something far beyond anything he had felt on Earth.

He turned to Sam and smiled, and Sam smiled back, his eyes twinkling.

They rowed back to the beach and started up the grill. Sam pulled out the ice chest and unwrapped three very green-looking sandwiches with sticky purple things coming out of them.

"Love them gollywhoggers," said Sam, as he threw them on the grill to cook.

The gollywhoggers sizzled and popped and smoked, and soon were grilled to a greenish purple brown. "Here, try one."

Jason stared at the gollywhogger. "It looks, uhhhh . . . delicious."

"Got at least six different tastes. You're bound to like some of them."

Jason nibbled at the gollywhogger. Did it taste like turnips? Onions? Not good. He took another bite. His mouth full, he grimaced at Sam, trying to smile. Then, ever so slowly, the gollywhogger began to taste like a hot dog with mustard. As he was getting used to that, it turned into guacamole and chips, which turned into spaghetti with meatballs.

"Hmmmmmmmmmmmm." This was getting good. He took another bite. Now it was apricot. Or was it peach?

Jason looked up from his eating and gave a start. Standing on the roof of the Dart was one of the chomper birds who had flown over the beach, looking very big and green and staring at Jason's gollywhogger with round purple eyes.

"Little beggars," said Sam. "They always come around when I cook gollywhoggers."

"He doesn't look little to me," said Jason.

The chomper hopped off the car and started to waddle toward Jason and his gollywhogger.

He backed away down the beach. "Shoo, bird, shoo."

"Here," said Sam, tossing the extra gollywhogger toward the bird, who opened his beak wide and caught it on the fly, then swallowed it whole.

"You don't know what you're missing if you don't

chew," said Sam to the chomper as Jason stepped back from the bird and finished off his gollywhogger, savoring a delicious hot fudge sundae with whipped cream and a cherry.

"Shoo, bird," he said again, wiping off his mouth, and then showing the bird his empty hands. The bird, seeing no more gollywhoggers, unfolded his enormous wings and took off across the lake.

Jason looked at his watch. "Sam, it's past two o'clock. We'll never get back in time!"

"Not to worry, kid."

"Sam, if we're late already, how can we get back in time?"

"On Earth, time is time, but when you're out in space going faster than light, time is not so rigid. More room to wiggle, so to speak."

"How can time not be the same everywhere?"

"Depends on how fast you go. If you go really fast and you use wormholes, then you can make time go faster or slower. Depends on how you fiddle with the space-time continuum when you're in a wormhole. Anyway, even on Earth time isn't rigid. Can't you fly from India to the U.S. and arrive before you left? You know, leave at noon on Friday and arrive an hour earlier on the same day? Happens all the time."

Sam packed up the barbecue. "If we choose the right speed and wormhole, we can be back at your house almost any time we want. Except in space travel there's a limit to how far back in time you can go. Can't get home before we left."

"How come?"

"Dunno. Haven't figured it out yet. I guess for now that time travel stuff is just science fiction."

As the Dart slowly rose up, Jason could see bongo fish swimming in the lake, their bright lights flashing. Then the Dart turned straight up to the sky, and in an instant, the planet was far behind them. Again the vast blackness of space was all around.

Jason looked at the map. "Look, here's Route 66, super-express lane. Let's try that."

Sam took a small black box out from under the dashboard and began to do calculations on its tiny keypad, muttering to himself, "Hmmmm, let's see, if we adjust speed to X minus 256 over 3,478, and the time is two thirty-four Universe Time, we should be okay. When did you say we have to be back in Berkeley?"

"Noon."

"That should do it," said Sam as he entered the time on the keypad and stuck it back under the dashboard.

He swerved the Dart to the left, and once again they were in a dark tunnel of a wormhole. When they popped out of the tunnel into the vastness of space, Sam turned on the intergalactic radio. Jason munched on a glazed doughnut. The humming of the car and the quiet music made him drowsy. His head fell back on the seat, and he slept, oblivious to the universe drifting by.

Jason woke to the *pop* of the car flying out of the wormhole. In front of them was Earth, with the moon behind it.

Home.

The Dart swooped down, and before Jason could finish stretching and yawning, they were on the ground, parked in the empty lot on Ninth Street.

As Jason climbed out of the Dart, he looked at his watch. "Yikes, it's ten after."

"Ooh, I guess we did cut it a little close. Darn time computer," said Sam, picking up the small black box and banging it with his hand. "Have to get somebody to look at it. Hasn't been working right for a while." He held it next to his head and shook it some more.

Jason stood looking at Sam and the Dart. Had the trip really happened? Jason's head was spinning, and he felt slightly dizzy. He smiled at Sam, wondering when he would see him again, but he didn't dare ask him. "So long."

"See ya, kiddo. Come and visit Edna and me sometime."

"Uh, yeah, sure." Jason smiled. He didn't quite know why, but this invitation from Sam made him happy, and he knew that somehow he would meet Edna.

Jason hurried toward the street. Sam called after him, "Or we'll drop in. . . ."

He turned to wave at Sam. "Anytime," he called out, then started up Ninth Street. At the end of the block, he looked up in time to see the Dart climb into the sky and disappear in a flash.

Jason felt as if everything was a faraway dream. The streets were the same, the houses were the same, the cars were the same, but somehow it was all distant and insubstantial. As he started for home, his feet hardly touched the ground.

Though Jason didn't notice it as he walked away, a black car with a whirling antenna was nearby, methodically driving down one street after another, back and forth, crisscrossing the area around the empty lot, finally arriving at the lot itself. The car slowed and then circled the lot, its antenna humming. It parked, but no one got out, and after a long time, it drove off.

Eleven

*L*uckily, Jason's mom's sense of time was as bad as the Dart's computer. She leaned into his room when she got home at twelve twenty. "Ready to go? We have to hurry."

On the way to soccer, Sputnik perched in the back seat. He liked to go to soccer games. In fact, he liked to go for any kind of expedition, and would even go on a walk with Jason, trailing behind him a few feet.

As they were driving up Hopkins toward the soccer field, Jason half expected his mother's Taurus wagon to float up into the air. He could still hear the rush of the

Dart moving through space, and the Earth seemed pale compared with the brilliance of the galaxies he had seen. He looked up at the sky. To think that it hid such wonders.

The soccer field was in King Park, and circling it was a running track, where people jogged in their little running shorts. To Jason they looked like ants on a treadmill. How could they run around that boring track, captive in their tiny minds, when the vast, beautiful universe was all around them? He wanted to cry out, "Wake up, everybody! Wake up! The cosmos is much bigger and more beautiful than you ever imagined!"

He was yanked out of these thoughts by the voice of his coach: "Jameson, what took you so long? You're late. Time to warm up."

Midway through the first half, the coach said to Jason, "You'll play goalie now. Remember, keep your eye on the ball, no matter where it is on the field."

Jason smiled at the coach. He was thinking about bongo fish.

The coach walked off to talk to some other kids.

The assistant coach came over. "Now, remember, keep your eye on the ball at all times, no matter what's going on."

Jason smiled at him and thought about bongo fish.

Fortunately, Jason's team was better than the other team, so most of the game was being played at the other end of the field. Jason's team, the Green Leeches, scored the first goal.

He stood in front of the goal, trying to keep his mind on the game and his eyes on the ball. bongo fish were swimming around his brain, and doughnut holes and gollywhoggers filled his taste buds. Jason looked up and saw a cloud drifting past. It looks exactly like a bongo fish, he thought. He remembered all the tricks the Bongo fish had done and became engrossed in the cloud floating by. It was such a beautiful cloud, and it looked so much like a bongo fish.

From far away it seemed like someone was calling to Jason. The calling grew louder, and suddenly he turned to face the field. Everyone was rushing toward him. The other team's center, a huge player with hairy legs, was dribbling the ball and bearing down on him ferociously. At the last second, the huge player kicked the ball straight for the far post. Jason dove as hard as he could, but the ball slipped past his hands and he slid on his chest across the muddy field.

"GOAL!" cried everyone on the other team.

As he picked himself up and brushed the dirt and grass off his shirt, Jason felt, for the first time since he had landed, as if he had come back to Earth. The other team was running in circles and high-fiving and jumping up and down. He could see his coach on the sidelines shaking his head, and he thought he heard the assistant coach say, "That boy is a million miles away." Jason wished he *were* a million miles away, or maybe even a million light-years away.

From then on, he made sure not to look up at the clouds, in case any bongo fish drifted by. The next time the ball came toward him, he was ready and caught it with ease. At halftime the coach took him out and he sat on the bench for the rest of the game.

"Hey, Jason, what's up?" His friend Joel sat down on the bench next to him, Joel with the glasses and the big frizzy hair. Joel didn't get much playing time either.

"Can't believe I missed that goal."

"Don't worry about it. Everybody spaces out sometimes."

That's the right word for it, thought Jason. He went back to thinking about bongo fish.

When they got home, his mother said, "By the way, I found this funny little card stuffed in the back pocket of your jeans when I went to wash them. Where is it from?"

"Uh, I found it on the street."

"An intergalactic garage?" She handed it to Jason. "Ahh, Berkeley."

Twelve

At school on Monday morning, Jason couldn't stop thinking about his strange adventure with Sam and the Dart. In first period, while Ms. Rothbar droned on about history and George Washington crossing a famous river during the American Revolution, Jason was thinking, What's the point of history? What good is it? All that matters is that I went to space. I didn't cross some dinky river. I crossed outer space, all the way to the Pleiades.

"Jason?" Ms. Rothbar was staring at him. "I asked you a question."

"Yes?"

" 'Yes' is not the answer. Did you even hear the question? Someone else?"

Julie Rotunda raised her hand. "The Delaware," she said with a smug expression.

"Yes, that is correct. Washington crossed the Delaware."

Jason wondered if he should tell someone at school about his adventure. Maybe his friend Joel. He was into strange stuff. He even had a weird old chemistry set in his basement, and he was always blowing things up with it.

As he and Joel sat at lunch eating their sandwiches, Jason said, "Do you think aliens are real? Like UFO aliens?"

"Why do you ask?"

"Well, I just, you know . . . I was kind of, I don't know, wondering about them."

"My dad thinks they're real. Haha. He's a little strange sometimes."

"Hmmmm."

When Jason got home, he sat down in front of Sputnik. "I mean, Sputs, what do you think? Are they real?"

Then he thought, What am I saying? What does a cat know?

Sputnik sneezed a small sneeze and looked intently at Jason. Jason stared back, looking deeply into his eyes.

Maybe cats did understand people.

He went on. "I think Sam must be real because if he wasn't, how could I—"

Sputnik sneezed again and walked out of the room and down the hall. He stood in front of his food bowl, looking at Jason. The bowl was empty.

Sputnik was hungry.

Maybe we really did go to the Pleiades, Jason thought as he opened a can of cat food.

A few weeks later, on a Monday night just after he fell asleep, Jason had a dream. A bad dream. He was standing in front of Ms. Rothbar's class, in pink underwear, trying to explain about Sam and the Dart. Ms. Rothbar was shining a bright light in his face.

"So, tell us, Jason, about these so-called aliens from outer space. Did they cross the Delaware?" She cackled a high-pitched laugh and pointed at Jason with a long, bony finger. Behind her everyone in class was laughing uproariously and pointing at him in his underwear. Jason tried to speak, but no words would come out, and the class was laughing louder and louder and banging on their desks with their pencils, *bang bang bang*, and then *tap . . . tap . . . tap.* Slowly Jason drifted up from the dream. What was that tapping? Where was it coming from?

He sat up in bed and turned around, then walked to the window and opened it. He leaned out and looked down. Nothing. He looked to the side. Nothing. He looked to the other side. Nothing. Then he craned his neck around and looked up. Sitting on the ledge above the window were two dark shapes. One of the shapes spoke.

"Hey, kid, how ya doin'?"

"Sam?" said Jason. "What are you doing here?"

"Dart ran out of gas. Gas gauge must be broke or something. Say, can we come inside?"

"Sure," said Jason, looking up at the other dark shape. It spoke.

"Whatcha gawking at, kid? Never seen an alien on a window ledge before?"

"Are you Edna?"

"Last time I checked."

"Glad to meet you."

"The pleasure's all mine," said Edna. "Now could we come inside? This ledge is killing my backside."

"You have to be quiet," Jason whispered. "My mom might still be awake." Sam and Edna climbed down off the ledge and into the room. Sam had on the same pair of jeans and the jacket he had worn before. Edna was shorter than Sam, with stocky legs and strong arms sticking out of a pink dress with green flowers on it. A pair of purple glasses with sparkling rims framed her lively eyes. Her skin was blue like Sam's, and her hair was slightly blue too, teased up into a pompadour and covered with a bright pink scarf. Like Sam, she was wearing purple high-top sneakers. She carried a large purse that was silvery and a little bit furry.

If Sam was a grandfatherly alien who knew cars, then Edna was a grandmother who could handle anything else. She looked around the room, and then turned to Jason, sizing him up intently. She reached out and pinched him on the arm.

"Doesn't anybody feed you anything?"

"Uh . . . my mom makes pretty good—"

"Oh, Edna, don't start in. You don't know hardly anything about these Earth people."

"Yes, I do, Sam. I read a book about Earth once. I know exactly what they eat."

"This kid looks plenty healthy to me. Speaking of food," said Sam, looking around, "got anything to eat? Hot chocolate or something? Haven't had a bite since Vega."

"Okay, but you have to stay in my room and be quiet. If my mom finds you, I'll be in major trouble."

"Don't worry," said Sam, sitting in a chair in the corner. Edna picked up a magazine from the floor and started reading it.

Jason opened the door a crack and peered down the hall. His mother's door was shut, but he could see a sliver of light at the bottom.

Gingerly, he tiptoed into the kitchen and pulled down a can of hot chocolate mix from the shelf. He took a quart of milk out of the refrigerator and poured some into a saucepan, to heat it up. As he was getting out a spoon, he dropped it, and his mother called out, "Jason, what are you doing in the kitchen?"

"Oh, nothing, Mom. Just making some hot chocolate."

He tiptoed back down the hall clutching the two mugs of hot chocolate tightly.

"Hmmm, looks good," said Sam. "Any marshmallows? Can't have hot chocolate without marshmallows."

"Oh, yeah, I forgot about you and marshmallows."

Jason tiptoed back to the kitchen. While he was reaching for the package of marshmallows at the back of the cabinet, a can of soup fell out and crashed to the floor.

"Jason Jameson, what in the world *are* you doing?" cried his mother from the other room.

He put on his calmest voice. "Getting some marshmallows, Mom. Everything under control here." He tiptoed back down the hall with the marshmallows and a bag of chocolate chip cookies. He handed the marshmallows to Sam, who squeezed three of them into his hot chocolate. Then he took one and flipped it high in the air and caught it in his mouth. Edna was interested in the chocolate chip cookies, and chomped loudly on two at once.

"Mmmm, that's more like it," Sam said, stirring his hot chocolate with his blue finger. "As I was saying, we ran into a little trouble with the Dart. Edna and I had been planning to take some vacation time and visit a few spots we'd never seen. Always wanted to see the Grand Canyon, didn't we, Edna?"

"What? Oh, yes, and Disney World. What about Las Vegas?"

"Someday, dear, someday." Sam turned to Jason. "She wants to see Elvis."

"Elvis Presley?"

"Isn't he wonderful? I love 'Heartbreak Hotel.'" Edna stood up and sang in a throaty voice, her arms spread wide, "Love me tender, love me do . . ."

"Didn't he die? Like in 1977 or something?" said Jason.

She stopped and looked at Jason. "Don't you believe it for a second, young man. I know Elvis is still alive somewhere in the cosmos. His music is all over, from Orion to Andromeda."

"He doesn't play Las Vegas anymore. I'm sure of that," said Sam, throwing a marshmallow up and catching it in his mouth.

"We'll see," said Edna, as she sat back down on Jason's bed. "I heard they found a miraculous picture of him on a potato chip. You can see it in a museum."

Chewing the marshmallow, Sam started again on his story. "Anyway, I was coming in for a perfect landing, heading straight for the Grand Canyon, when halfway through the upper atmosphere, I discover we're low on gas. Big problem. I couldn't keep my angle, got off course, and ended up coming in over San Jose."

"You should have checked the gas before we left, dear."

"Then I get an idea."

"No, Sam, it was my idea. I said, 'Sam, what about that smart kid you met? Let's go find him.'"

"Why couldn't you stop at a gas station?" said Jason.

Edna looked at Jason over the top of her sparkling glasses. "See, kid, the Dart doesn't run on Earth gas. Petroleum products are long gone on our planet. Besides, our credit cards don't work here."

Sam continued, "So I land as smooth as mashed potatoes on the 880 freeway on-ramp, heading north."

"I didn't think it was all that smooth," said Edna.

Sam paid no attention and went on with his story. "We merged onto the freeway with the rest of the workaday world and headed north to Berkeley. People looked at us kind of funny, but Edna waved and gave them a big smile."

Jason peered out the window. "Where's the Dart now?"

"Gettin' to that part. By the time we got to San Leandro, the gas was almost gone. So I got off the freeway and pulled into the first lot I saw. Used car lot or something. Anyway, there were lots of old cars in it."

"Are you sure it was a used car lot?"

"Pretty sure. There was a big crane in the back."

"How did you get here?"

Edna peered over the top of her glasses again. "Stuck ourselves to the back of a bus with some superglue."

"Really?"

Sam and Edna looked at each other and laughed.

"Took a cab. He talked our ear off about the science fiction book he's writing. I wanted to tell him what outer space is like, but Edna said maybe we should keep quiet. He liked the Pleiades money we paid him. Gave him all the change we had."

Edna looked around the room. "Can we stay a couple of days?"

"Here?"

"You want us to sleep outside with the pigeons?"

"Maybe you could sleep under the bed."

Edna leaned down. "I'm not getting under there with those dirty socks."

"How about the closet?" said Sam.

"Any dirty socks?" Edna looked skeptically at Jason.

"A few."

"This is more than a few." She began to throw socks and dirty underwear out of the closet. "It'll do. We could sleep on the shelves."

Jason dug around for blankets and sheets and made up beds for Sam and Edna on the shelves of the closet. He tucked them in and started to shut the door.

"Please . . . I have claustrophobia," said Edna.

Jason left the door open, got into bed, and turned the light out.

"Good night, Sam."

"Good night, Jason."

"Good night, Edna."

"Good night, Jason."

He lay awake in the dark, listening. He could hear Sam's breath slowing down and Edna falling asleep. Sam's breathing turned into a delicate snore, a sort of quiet whistling. Then, bit by bit, it grew louder. It wasn't like anything Jason had heard before—there were lots of little clicks and whistles and *chugga-chugga*s. Soon the snoring turned so loud that it rattled the door of the closet. Jason pulled his pillow over his ears.

What would happen if his mother came in and found two slightly blue aliens asleep in the closet? There might be all sorts of terrible outcomes. He knew he should be worried, but mostly he was tired. He drifted off too, with his pillow still wrapped around his ears.

Thirteen

"Jason, time to get up." The sun was streaming in the window, and his mother was standing in the doorway.

Rubbing his eyes, he sat up. There at the foot of the bed was Sam's cap.

"How cute," said his mother. "Where did that come from?"

"Uh, I found it at the park."

"What's that sound?" said his mother. Sam was still snoring.

When she wasn't looking, Jason flipped on the radio.

"Turn that down, it's too loud," said his mother.

"Can't turn my radio alarm off."

His mother went out the door, muttering to herself.

Sam and Edna climbed out of the closet.

"What's all the racket?"

"Shhhhhh. . . . You gotta be quiet."

Jason's mother leaned back into the room.

Edna and Sam froze behind the door.

"Jason, are you okay?"

"Fine, Mom."

"I left some cereal out for you," she yelled as she went off to work. "Have a good day at school! And fix that radio."

Jason turned the radio off.

"You have school today?" asked Sam. "Too bad, because we need you. How about after school you give us a hand with making some gas for the Dart?"

"Me?" Jason thought, How can a Berkeley kid help someone from the Pleiades make rocket fuel?

"Like I said, the Dart doesn't run on Earth gas. It runs on intergalactic rocket fuel."

"Isn't rocket fuel superexplosive and hard to get hold of?"

"Not *that* kind of rocket fuel. Our fuel is much safer, and a *lot* more powerful. We can cook it up right here."

"In the kitchen? What if my mom finds us?"

"We'll do it when she's asleep. It's pretty nontoxic."

Jason didn't like the sound of "pretty nontoxic." It

sounded like "mildly radioactive" or "slightly flesh-eating."

"In the Pleiades we make fuel out of things you've never heard of, but on Earth you can make a pretty good version out of bubblegum and green vegetables and some other stuff."

"Bubblegum?"

"You cook it up with baking soda and Gatorade, then you put it into the portable atom smasher, and out comes rocket fuel."

"Portable atom smasher? I thought atom smashers were huge."

"Not ours," said Edna, patting her purse. "I always carry one."

"The smasher breaks everything into free-range atoms," Sam said, "and then puts them back together into hyper-fuel for Dart spaceships. You can put almost anything into the smasher. I was stuck out near Orion once, and I made fuel out of a two-week-old pepperoni pizza I found under the seat."

They went into the kitchen and opened the refrigerator. A wilted head of broccoli moldered at the back.

"Our first ingredient," said Jason. "And I won't have to eat it."

"Speaking of ingredients," said Edna, smiling at Jason, "where's breakfast?"

Jason pointed to the cereal and milk on the kitchen table.

"I love Cheerios," said Sam, crunching the cereal loudly.

While Sam and Edna were eating, Jason went to his room and came back with a drawing he had made at school.

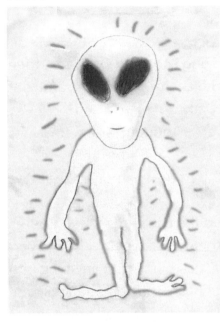

Sam looked at the picture, then at Jason. "Friend of yours?"

Jason laughed. "It seems like everybody here on Earth thinks that aliens look like this picture. Little green men with big weird eyes and a tiny mouth."

"Yeah, those guys," Sam said. "I know exactly who you're talking about."

"They're all over the universe," said Edna, wiping her mouth off with a napkin.

"You don't look like that," said Jason.

"I sure hope not," said Edna. "I'd jump off a cliff if I did."

"I can't remember exactly what galaxy they came from, but now they're all over the place," said Sam.

"Like rats or something," said Edna.

"It's their attitude that gets on my nerves," said Sam.

"They're all wacko scientists. All they do is snivel around the universe, abducting people and doing experiments on them, stealing cows, burning holes in the ground. Like nine-year-olds with a chemistry set. No offense, kid."

"They give me the creeps," said Edna.

"Remember that time, honey, out on that planet, what was it called?"

"Don't remind me, Sam."

"We were on a nice little vacation when this alien spaceship comes sneaking up and stops right above us. Little guys like in your picture come down a ladder and look at us with those creepy eyes. Then they start talking in unintelligible green-men language.

"All of a sudden, they grab Edna and me and haul us into their spaceship. Before we know what's happening, they strap me down on some kind of operating table and they're pulling out their little operating tools and they've got this strange glint in their eyes.

"When Edna saw me on the operating table, she really lost it. Pulled some Pleiades karate moves on those guys and had them up against the wall in no time, their little green teeth chattering away. Said if they didn't let us go she'd take a phaser cannon and blow their dinky spaceship out of the sky."

Edna cracked a smile. "You should have seen their little green faces. They bowed and scraped and begged our pardon and got off that planet pretty quick."

Jason looked at Sam and Edna, his mouth open. "You mean these guys are real? And they really do abduct people? I thought those were just stories made up by weirdos."

"Yeah, they're real," said Edna, "but don't worry your brain about it too much. They've been to Earth so many times, I'm sure they're getting bored by now. Little green men have very short attention spans, at least that's what I've heard."

Jason wasn't sure if that was a reason to feel reassured or not.

Edna got up and wandered around the kitchen, opening all the cupboards and tasting things. "Hmmm, okay . . . interesting stuff . . . Hmmm . . . delicious. Hey, look, here's some baking soda."

Jason glanced at the clock on the wall. "Time for school."

"On the way home, could you get the rocket fuel stuff? Like thirty-six pieces of gum and a bottle of Gatorade?"

"What flavor of Gatorade? And what about the bubble-gum?"

"The green Gatorade, and any kind of pink bubble-gum that's super chewy. And don't work too hard at school."

Fourteen

"*L*ot of bubblegum," said the man at the Cedar Market, when Jason piled the thirty-six pieces on the counter that afternoon. "Are you going to chew it all yourself?"

"No, it's for a science experiment at school."

"Gatorade for the experiment, too?"

Jason smiled and picked up the bubblegum and the bottle of Gatorade and headed home.

Sam was taking a nap in the closet, and Edna was sitting on Jason's bed, reading a magazine, eating a bag of potato chips, and occasionally stroking Sputnik, who sat on her lap quietly.

She looked up. "Hi, kid, how ya doin'? Found your cat inside my purse this afternoon, sound asleep. He seems to like it in there. Skinny little guy. Are you sure he's okay?"

Jason looked down at Sputnik. "He's fine. Maybe he doesn't like that new cat food Mom bought for him." As he said this, he thought, What if he *is* sick? He wondered whether Edna knew how to cure diseases. She was from an advanced civilization, after all.

Slipping into the kitchen after Jason's mother had gone to bed that night, Sam, Edna, and Jason quietly shut the door behind them and laid out the ingredients for the rocket fuel. Sam picked up the bubblegum.

"Now we chew."

They divided up the thirty-six pieces of bubblegum, so each had twelve pieces, and one by one stuffed them into their mouths.

"You loog like a chibmunk," said Edna to Jason.

"You're dwooling," said Jason to Edna.

"Tages a while to ged it going," said Sam. Edna seemed to have very strong jaws and chomped loudly and vigorously.

"Aaargghhh," said Jason. He liked chewing gum, but twelve pieces was ten too many. His jaws ached.

"Aaargghhh," said Sam.

After a long time chewing, they took the gum out and laid it on the table. "Okay, now we cook it up."

They mixed the bubblegum and the broccoli in a pot on the stove, and Jason started stirring. "It looks like someone's brains."

"My brains don't look like that," said Edna, looking sideways at Jason.

The more Jason stirred, the stickier the broccoli and bubblegum got.

"This'll make it easier," Sam said, splashing Gatorade freely into the pot.

"Hey, not on my shirt," said Jason.

"No problem, kid—we'll clean it up later. Time for the baking soda."

"A teaspoon or half a teaspoon?" said Edna. "No, wait, I think it's three tablespoons. Yes, three tablespoons. I'm sure of it."

Jason carefully measured out three tablespoons of baking soda and added them to the pot.

The pot gurgled and bubbled like a live creature.

"Maybe we should add a little oil," Sam said, reaching for a bottle in the cupboard. He poured it into the pot.

Suddenly the pot bubbled up. Fizzling and gurgling, it spilled over the stove and down onto the kitchen floor, covering the linoleum with green slime.

"What was in that bottle?" said Jason.

"Cooking oil," Sam said, peering at the label. "Oh . . . actually, it's . . . uh . . . vinegar."

"Vinegar!" cried Jason. "Don't you know? Vinegar and baking soda is what you use in a science experiment to make a volcano!"

"Sorry about that."

"Sam never reads labels."

Jason looked around the kitchen. "Now what?"

"We scrape it up and put it in the atom smasher."

"Hon, have you got the smasher?"

"Somewhere in here," she said, opening her purse.

"Uh-oh," said Sam.

Edna began to look through her purse. Out came a bright green cell phone, a large red makeup kit, a pair of sandals, and a hairbrush. Then a pair of pliers, two screwdrivers, four Band-Aids, and what looked like a package of purple spaghetti.

She straightened up and wiped a bead of sweat off her brow. "I know I put it in here."

She dove back in. A sandwich, a bottle of pills, a mousetrap, purple stockings, and a cookie flew out. Then what looked like a tiny welding kit and a small saw clunked onto the kitchen floor. Jason peeked over Edna's shoulder into the purse. At first he couldn't see anything, but then his eyes grew wide. On the outside it looked like a regular purse, but inside it was much bigger. Instead of a small space, Edna was reaching into a vast interior world, pulling objects out of nothingness. It was as if she were materializing everything out of thin air, a universe that was somehow contained within the small space of the purse. He stepped back.

"That's some purse. How much can it hold?"

"Lots, believe me, lots," said Edna. "Oh, here it is." She reached her whole arm deep into the purse and pulled out a shiny chrome object shaped like a coffee grinder. It was a cylinder with an aluminum cap and bottom, and a clear plastic middle you could see into. An electrical cord dangled from one end.

Setting it on the floor, Sam carefully spooned the green mixture into the smasher.

"That should do it," he said, screwing on the top.

"Here, put these on." Edna pulled out dark glasses. "Gets real bright when the smasher gets going."

"Could you plug it in?" asked Sam.

Gingerly, Jason put the plug in the outlet.

Rrrrrrrrrrrrrrrrrrrrrrr. . . . The machine began to whir, quietly at first and then a little louder. The container inside whirled around, faster and faster. At first there was a dull glow, but it got brighter and brighter as the machine spun faster. Jason stared in fascination.

Soon the atom smasher lit the kitchen with a blazing radiance. Jason could no longer see the green, only a bright, glowing mass that etched everything in the room with the brilliance of a spotlight. Even with dark glasses on, it was almost too bright. The whole kitchen seemed to be disappearing in a blaze of white.

Suddenly the room was plunged into darkness, and the atom smasher fizzled and went out.

"Wha—what happened?" said Jason.

"It's done," said Sam.

The smasher hiccuped. The mixture inside had turned smooth and milky white.

Sam poured it out into a bottle and screwed the top on. "Looks like A-plus fuel to me. Off to the Grand Canyon, eh, Edna?"

"Finally we can start our vacation."

They looked around at the kitchen.

"Hmmmm," said Sam.

"Hmmmm," said Edna. "Kind of a disaster area."

They all took paper towels and started wiping up the floor. In the middle of wiping, Jason turned and asked Sam, "Where did you say you left the Dart?"

"Something like A-1 Demonstration or Auto Detail."

Jason turned around and stared at Sam. Suddenly a terrible thought dawned in his mind. A thought almost too awful to think.

Sam went on, "I'm sure it said 'auto demonstration' or something. It was hard to see in the dark."

"Quick, what was the address?"

Sam looked at the back of his hand. "22451 Alvarado, San Leandro."

Jason ran to his mother's computer and typed in the address. He tapped his foot as he waited for the dilapidated machine to respond. The computer wheezed and then the screen went blank. Jason pounded on the keyboard, and as the screen came back on, he froze, his hand in midair, eyes staring in disbelief.

"Sam, it's . . . it's . . ."

"What's the matter?"

"It's an auto demolition yard! Sam, that's where they crush cars into little cubes and melt them down!"

Sam turned pale and sagged against the kitchen table.

Edna gasped and dropped her purse. "It can't be. . . ."

They stood looking at each other, fear in their eyes.

"Let's go!" Sam said.

"Wait. It's way down in San Leandro," Jason said. "It would take hours to walk. I don't know how to drive my mom's car, and I don't have enough money for a taxi. We'll have to take a bus."

Jason rummaged through a drawer in the kitchen.

"Here's a bus map." He unfolded it on the floor and they pored over it. "Okay, so we can take the 96 to Oakland, and then it goes down Fourteenth Street to Thirty-sixth. We have to walk from there."

"What about the kitchen?" said Edna, throwing things back in her purse.

"It'll have to wait. We'll lose the Dart if we don't hurry," said Jason.

He ran to his room and brought out three hooded sweatshirts.

"Not too stylish, kid," said Edna, holding one at arm's length.

"It's cold out," said Jason. "You can pull the hoods up and no one will see your blueness. Everybody on Earth wears them."

"Is our blueness that bad?" said Edna, brushing a strand of hair out of her eyes.

"Your blueness is fine. It's just that you're from 410 light-years away."

The three of them climbed out Jason's window, tip-toed down the fire escape, and walked the few blocks to University Avenue as fast as they could. Usually the buses were slow and unreliable. You could wait an hour for the right one and then three in a row would go by one after the other.

Tonight they were lucky. In minutes they were seated in the 96 bus, three small figures with faces looking out from hooded sweatshirts. Jason tapped his foot nervously. What if Sam and Edna had to stay on Earth forever?

They stared at the world outside the bus, their faces tight with worry.

As the bus was pulling away from Ashby Avenue, Jason looked up to see a policeman walking down the aisle.

Jason signed to Sam and Edna to pull their hoods down. Slowly the officer made his way along the aisle. He seemed to be looking everyone over. Was he looking for aliens? Was he a special kind of investigator on the watch for extraterrestrial invaders? Jason stared at the floor. The policeman strolled past their seat and sat at the back. Jason sneaked a look and saw that he wasn't a policeman at all, but a security guard with an ACE Co. badge on his uniform. Not a real policeman at all. Just a rent-a-cop!

They sat silently as the bus crawled along the streets, winding deeper and deeper into nighttime Oakland. They were almost the only passengers. Jason looked around the bus. Among the signs for computer academies and English-language schools he saw a strange ad that someone had scribbled graffiti on.

"What does it say?" said Sam, watching Jason read the ad.

"It says that people who don't like aliens have a hard time sleeping."

"That's for sure," said Edna. "I had nightmares for a month after we met those little green guys on our vacation."

"I slept fine after I met you guys," said Jason. "Except when you snored, Sam."

Sam smiled.

What an odd name, thought Jason. Effrem Zimburger. I wonder where he's from?

Fifteen

"*H*ere!" Jason said when they came to East Thirty-sixth. They jumped up and scrambled out the back door. A single streetlamp on the corner cast an eerie light. Walking close together, they crossed Fourteenth Street and started down a side street, looking over their shoulders as they went. This was the kind of neighborhood Jason's mother always warned him about. The lights were far apart, and the streets were gloomy, with long shadows stretching across the rutted pavement. There were no houses, only graffiti-covered warehouses and abandoned cars lying next to piles of trash.

Jason pulled the hood tight over his head and walked as quickly as he could. Sam and Edna had to jog on their short legs to keep up. A low-slung black car with shiny hubcaps drove past them very slowly but didn't stop.

"Nervous?" Sam called out to Jason in front of him.

"A little," said Jason.

"Here, check this out," said Sam.

Jason walked back to Sam, who had stopped under a streetlight and was pulling something metallic out of his pocket. It looked like a water pistol but a little more serious. The trigger glowed.

"Ray gun," said Sam. "All aliens carry a ray gun."

"Really? I thought that was only in the movies."

"These ray guns do a lot more than movie ray guns."

Edna muttered, "I hate ray guns."

"I took that safety class, honey. I know what I'm doing."

Sam showed him the dial on the back of the ray gun. "See? It does all kinds of stuff."

Jason read the writing around the dial.

In the middle it said: X-O-ZAPPO RAY GUN. SINCE THE YEAR 10,856.

Around the dial, starting at the top:

1. Burn small hole
2. Burn large hole
3. Temp. vaporize
4. Mushymooshy

5. Cook oatmeal
6. Stun toads
7. Create universe (DANGER: USE SETTING WITH CAUTION!)

"Want to see how it works?" Sam said.

"Right now?"

"Yeah, sure."

Sam set the dial to "Burn small hole" and then he began to play with the ray gun as if he were a cowboy.

"Stop fooling around," said Edna.

He twirled the ray gun, flipped it from hand to hand, put it behind his back, and then quickly pulled it out.

"No fancy stuff!" cried Edna, just as Sam was bringing it out from behind his back. The ray gun caught on his jacket, and pointing down, it went off. *Zzzzzzzttt!* A bright yellow light flashed out of the ray gun and straight into the toe of Jason's shoe.

"Ow!" A small puff of smoke rose up from the shoe. Jason hopped around, holding on to his foot.

"I'm so sorry," said Sam.

"Told you," said Edna.

Jason took off his shoe and sock and wiggled his toes. "At least it only put a hole in the shoe and not my foot. It was pretty hot, though!"

"Jeez, kid, I feel terrible. I . . . I . . . don't know what got into me," said Sam.

"Glad you didn't put it on 'Burn large hole,'" said Jason.

"When will you ever grow up?" Edna looked at Sam in the dim light.

"Maybe I should carry the ray gun from now on," said Jason, feeling for a moment like a parent to this occasionally absentminded alien from an advanced civilization.

Jason tied his shoe and Sam helped him up and they started off again.

Soon they came to Alvarado Street. There, in front of them, were rows and rows of very decrepit-looking cars. A big sign in front of the gate said

A-1 DEMOLITION
TWENTY-FOUR-HOUR WRECKING.
YOU BRING IT. WE CRUSH IT.

Edna held her head in her hands.

"Guess I don't know how to read too good," said Sam glumly.

"I'm sure the Dart is okay," said Jason, as brightly as he could. "You only parked it yesterday."

Although the sign said "twenty-four-hour wrecking," there didn't seem to be anybody around.

The hulks of rusted-out, broken-down cars were piled all around them in long rows that stretched into the dark.

They walked up and down the rows, looking for the Dart.

Edna plodded behind Jason and Sam. Every so often she said "my feet hurt" or "my bunions are killing me."

"Just a little farther, honey. It's around here somewhere," Sam said. "I think it was next to a pink Cadillac."

The rows seemed to go on forever. Then Jason pointed. "That looks like something pink down there." They hurried toward it, Edna trailing behind.

"This is where I left the Dart, I'm sure of it," Sam said. "Next to that car."

They stopped in their tracks, mouths open. The space next to the pink Cadillac was empty.

"It can't be," Sam said softly. He sat on the fender of the Cadillac and put his head in his hands.

Edna stood with a stricken look on her face. Jason felt as if he was about to cry.

A cold wind was blowing off the bay, and the dark seemed to close in around the three forlorn figures in the middle of the wrecking yard.

Jason looked at Sam and Edna. The Dart was probably crushed flat, maybe even melted down already.

They would never be able to get back to their planet. How could they survive on Earth?

They couldn't live in Jason's closet forever.

Sixteen

"It's gone," Sam said blankly.

"You didn't know it was a wrecking yard?"

"I guess I wasn't paying attention," said Sam. "I thought it was a parking lot."

Edna sat down next to him on the bumper of the pink Cadillac. She put her arm around his shoulders. "It's okay, honey. We'll get back to the Pleiades somehow."

After a long while, they stood up and started back toward the street.

As they walked, they heard the sound of machinery nearby.

Next to the parking lot was a high fence, which stretched all the way across the wrecking yard. Beyond the fence were bright lights—and something moving.

"What's in there?" asked Sam.

Jason shrugged. "Climb on my shoulders. Maybe you can see what's going on."

Sam peered over the fence. "Looks like some kind of crane, a really big crane."

"Do you see any cars?" asked Jason.

"Hmmmm, let's see. Oh, yes, there's some. . . . The crane is picking up an old car with a huge magnet, and then it's putting it in the big box and then— Oh, yikes! It's crushing the car! And . . . and . . . and THE DART IS NEXT IN LINE!"

Sam teetered back, and Jason staggered. He tried to grab on to the fence but missed, and they fell to the ground.

"Quick, the ray gun!" said Jason.

Sam pulled the ray gun out and set it on "Burn large hole." Aiming wildly at the fence, he pulled the trigger. *BOOM!* The fence shook, and there was smoke everywhere.

When the smoke cleared, there was a hole big enough for the three of them to climb through.

"Run!" cried Jason. The ominous shape of the crane

turned toward the Dart. Scurrying between the rows of cars, they reached the Dart, all by itself under the huge crane. Sam threw himself in the driver's side, and Jason and Edna dashed to the other side. The huge magnet hanging down from the crane lurched closer.

Sam was pushing buttons all over the dashboard. "Hit the green one!" he cried to Jason. "Now the red! Hang on to your hat, kid. Pedal to the metal, here we go!"

A rumble, a flash of rockets, and with a violent start, the Dart shot ahead just as the crane's magnet swooped toward the car. The car curved up and around the tower where the crane operator sat. As they roared past, Jason saw him frozen in his chair, mouth wide open, eyes bulging. Edna leaned out the window and waved. The operator looked as if he was about to fall out of his chair.

"Like a stunned mullet," Sam said.

The Dart soared up and away from the wrecking yard.

Sam laughed, heading the Dart farther into the nighttime sky.

Suddenly the car sputtered, backfired, and began to lose altitude.

"Forgot to put the fuel in!" cried Sam.

"Where can we land?"

They scanned the city below.

"There!" cried Jason, pointing to an empty parking lot by the bay, lit by arc lights.

As the Dart flew down toward the ground, it lurched violently, shuddering like a bucking bronco.

"We're down to the last drop," said Sam.

Jason grabbed the dashboard. Edna held on to Jason's arm while Sam worked frantically to control the Dart.

Instead of slowing down, the car seemed to be gaining momentum as it streaked toward the ground.

"No gas means we've got no gravity reducers. Have to come in on manual. Hold on to the steering wheel, kid."

Jason grabbed the steering wheel and held tight, while Sam frantically fiddled with dials and knobs. The Dart was going faster and faster, pitching wildly back and forth. Jason saw the ground filling the windshield and braced himself against the dashboard, expecting a terrible impact.

At the last second, the Dart pulled up and landed with a loud *thump* in the parking lot. Sam let out a sigh. Jason sat back, his heart pounding.

"Not such a bad landing, eh?" Sam said. "You got the gas?"

Jason felt in his pocket. It wasn't there. He felt in his other pocket. He twisted around and looked on the back seat, then by his feet. Paper cups, candy wrappers, and stale potato chips spilled out from under the seat, and there, among them, was the jar of fuel.

He groped through the mess and handed the bottle to Sam. "Lotta junk under that seat."

"If I've told him once, I've told him a thousand times," said Edna.

"I'll get to it next weekend. Really."

Sam climbed out of the car and unscrewed the gas cap. As he pulled it off, a puff of smoke came out. "We really were on empty."

Hopping back in, he started the Dart once more.

"Hey," said Edna, "let's go flying." She started singing. "Flyyyy me to the mooooooon. . . ."

Jason looked at Sam. "A trip to the Pleiades?"

"Maybe more of a local sightseeing trip," Sam said. "Kind of late to start out across the universe. How about beautiful San Francisco by night? The city tour."

"Who's the tour guide?" asked Jason.

"You."

They grinned at Jason. Edna thumped him on the back.

Jason folded his hand and held it close to his mouth as if he was gripping a microphone.

"Hmmmm. . . . Like this?" He made his voice as deep as he could: "Welcome to the fabulous San Francisco night tour. No matter what planet you're from, you'll find lots to love about our city! So let's get started! On our left is beautiful San Francisco Bay."

Sam swung the Dart in a big circle across the water. They were high above the bay now, the moon shining brightly. Jason looked down as they flew over the Bay Bridge. The cars below looked like tiny ants with headlights, creeping along the roadway.

"On our right, the spectacular Bay Bridge," said Jason,

still in his football announcer voice. "Say, folks, do you know which bridge is longer, the Bay Bridge or the Golden Gate?"

Sam looked at Jason. "Nope."

"We'll have the answer to that question later in the tour. Now it's time to hit the high spots of the big city." Jason went back to his regular voice. "Sam, can the people on the bridge see us?"

"No-See-Um paint on the bottom of the Dart. Just put it on last week."

"It's magic?"

"Sends the light in another direction. Something like that. I didn't quite understand when the Pleiades hardware store guy explained it, but it was on sale for only a goblek ninety-nine a gallon."

"How come you only painted the underside?"

"What? Ruin twenty-six coats of hand-rubbed, lime-green paint? We just painted the bottom, and then Edna took it up for a test drive, so I could see if it worked. Dart was completely invisible from below, but then Edna darn near took the roof off the garage when she tried to land it."

"I did not."

They were flying over Treasure Island, and soon the Ferry Building in San Francisco came into view.

Now they were floating directly above the city's skyscrapers, which reached toward them like giant stacks of Legos. A few lights were on in the offices, but otherwise the buildings loomed darkly into the sky. Far below, the empty streets glowed orange in the street-lights. Cars passed under the lights and then into darkness again, and the sidewalks were empty.

Jason pointed ahead. "Look over there."

He held his fist close to his mouth again. "Straight ahead, one of the wonders of the western United States, the Transamerica Pyramid. Not like the ones in Egypt—it's actually an office building, but it's really tall and pointed at the top."

"Can we land on the top?" asked Sam.

"No way, Sam. It's a point! We'd never get off. We'd be stuck like James and the giant peach on the Empire State Building!"

Sam swooped the Dart around the top of the pyramid in a big arc. Jason laughed as they circled lazily. It seemed close enough to touch.

He went back to his tour guide voice. "Now it's time for Fisherman's Wharf. We won't see a lot of fish from up here this time of night. Haha. Look, there's Alcatraz Island out in the middle of the bay. Wave hello to Al Capone, folks!"

"Who's Al Capone?" asked Edna.

"Long story," said Jason. "Just another bad joke from your tour guide. . . . But wait, straight ahead is the Golden Gate Bridge!" Jason thought for a moment and then, with excitement in his eyes, he said, "Now the highlight of our tour, the Golden Gate Bridge fly-under, a hundred miles an hour and only ten feet off the water!"

"A hundred miles an hour? Ten feet? That sounds too close for comfort."

"Oh, come on, Sam, can we do it? Please? It would be really cool."

"Gonna get me in trouble, kid."

"Fly the Golden Gate with Sam and Edna from the Pleiades! Bring 'er in low!" Jason pointed toward the bridge.

Sam swung the Dart down toward the bay, and soon they were tearing along just above the water.

Jason held on tight. The Dart roared past Alcatraz and out toward the bridge.

"Wow," said Jason, "this is close. Cool. Really great, really—SAM! WATCH OUT! Freighter dead ahead!"

Sam jerked the wheel to the left, and the Dart roared past the huge bow of the ship.

"Watch where you're going," said Edna, her arm braced against the dash.

The great red-orange Golden Gate Bridge came up fast, looming above them in the night sky. The lights of the roadway shone down onto the water, and the towers seemed to stretch higher than a skyscraper. The Dart whizzed above the water, like some strange water bug, rockets flaring, engine throbbing. They roared under the huge structure and out over the Pacific Ocean. Jason looked back to see the city's lights glowing magically over the water.

Sam slowed the Dart and turned south, and they rode in silence along the coast, the waves breaking against the shore below, the only sound the quiet humming of the car. Jason remembered his father taking him and his mother for a drive at night when he was little. "Let's get lost," his father used to say, and then he would drive them to somewhere they had never been before, somewhere magical and mysterious in the night. He remembered the feeling of coziness and security in the big car, the dashboard lights glowing, the engine purring softly, and his father at the wheel. Slowly he grew sleepy, and his head rested on Edna's shoulder.

The Dart floated over the ocean in the moonlight, and Sam leaned back in his seat with one hand on the wheel, humming a tune to himself. Jason sighed in his sleep.

Edna pointed at Jason, asleep between them. "Time to take this kid home to bed," she whispered.

"Long day. We need to get home. Grand Canyon trip will have to be some other time." Sam swung the Dart back up along the coast and then high above San Francisco and over the bay toward Berkeley.

They drifted gently down to Jason's apartment. The Dart hovered silently outside the window.

"Hey, kiddo, time to climb in your own bed," Edna

whispered to Jason. He slowly stirred, stretched, and woke up.

"Where are we?"

"Home."

"In space?"

"No, your home, right here on Earth. Good old Berkeley."

He climbed out of the Dart and through his bedroom window.

Edna and Sam leaned out the window of the Dart.

"By the way," asked Edna, "which bridge is longer?"

"That's easy," said Jason. "It's the Bay Bridge. It's really two bridges. But the Golden Gate is nicer looking."

Edna smiled at him. "So long. You ever need to get in touch with us, just call that number on Sam's card. Or you can use this." Once again she reached deep into her purse. "Let's see, where was that thing? Oh, here it is."

She pressed a metal box about the size of a bar of soap into his hand. It was smooth and cool to the touch.

Jason turned it over. "How do I . . . ?"

The Dart vibrated gently as it rose up, its lights winking on and off.

Edna waved out the open window of the Dart. "It's a Confabulator. You'll figure it out."

Jason watched the Dart rise higher into the sky, and then in a flash it was gone. He turned and climbed into bed, too tired to put on his pajamas, the Confabulator clutched in his hand.

As the Dart began its long flight home, Sam stared intently at one of the dials on the dashboard.

"What is it, honey?" said Edna.

"Detection scanner picked up something. Like maybe somebody was watching us on radar back in Berkeley."

"Hmm," said Edna. "Maybe it's a bug in the software. I'm going to take a nap. You drive safely now." She leaned back in her seat.

"I don't know, dear . . ."

The only reply was a loud snore.

Seventeen

*J*ason had heard the expression "smoke coming out of your ears," but he had never known what it meant until his mother came into his room the next morning. She stood in the doorway, her arms folded across her chest, staring angrily at him. He opened one eye to look at her. Why is she so angry? he thought.

Then he remembered the kitchen and the broccoli and the bubblegum and the vinegar and the baking soda.

His mother's foot was tapping on the floor.

"Jason, come with me."

Barefoot in his pajamas, hair tousled and eyes half open, he walked to the kitchen behind his mother. She glared at him, then swept her arm in an arc that encompassed the whole kitchen.

"*What is this?* What were you doing in here last night? What were you *thinking*?"

Jason rubbed his eyes. The mess was far worse than it had seemed the night before. There was green gunk everywhere: on the walls, the windows, the door of the refrigerator, the kitchen cabinets. It covered the top of the stove and dribbled down the front and probably filled the oven as well. He could feel his feet sticking to the squishy floor.

He looked at the sink. Not only were the dishes from last night's dinner not done, but most of them were coated with a layer of green goo that looked as if it had hardened overnight. Jason doubted that any dishwasher in the world would be able to get them clean. They didn't have a dishwasher anyway.

"Uh, actually . . ." Jason sighed. There was nothing to be done. Sam and Edna had been saved from being trapped on Earth forever, the lime-green Dart with the twenty-six coats of paint had been rescued by the narrowest of margins, and Jason would have to clean up the mess.

His mother looked around the room. Suddenly her

eyes stopped at something she hadn't seen before. She walked over and picked it up.

"And *what* is a pair of purple women's stockings doing in the kitchen?"

Jason sighed. They were Edna's. He stood in front of his mother, feeling small and uncomfortable. His hand twisted the sleeve of his pajamas into a tight knot. He felt a blush coming on, and then his mind wandered to Sam and Edna, somewhere far out in space in their cozy little house in the Pleiades, the Dart in the garage, the sprinkler watering the lawn.

Before he knew what he was doing, before he had time to think, he said what he'd never thought he would say:

"It was aliens, Mom, aliens."

"What?"

"It was aliens. They came in a spaceship."

"Right," said his mother. "And little green men are landing in Golden Gate Park to take over the world? Don't think, young man, that you're going to get out of this that easily. I've heard some lame excuses, but that is the lamest."

"No, really, it was aliens. Their names are Sam and Edna. They come from the Pleiades. In outer space."

"Outer space? Are you saying something about UFOs? Jason, this is NO TIME TO BE FOOLING WITH ME."

"I'm not fooling. They're real."

"Jason, aliens aren't real. They don't exist. They're only in science fiction stories."

Jason looked down at his feet. "These aliens are real, Mom. I saw them myself. They're—"

Jason's mother knelt in front of him. She looked into his eyes and held his hands. "You saw aliens?"

"We were making rocket fuel for their spaceship. That's why the kitchen is such a mess."

"You're pretending, right? Like you used to do when you were five?"

"No, Mom, they're real."

"Why would you think that? You must be under a lot of stress at school, dear."

He wasn't under a lot of stress at school. He liked school, and he liked recess a lot. The only part of school he didn't like was when Ms. Rothbar started talking about how great her pets were. Or when she talked about computers, or something else she knew nothing about.

"You *are* having a hard time—I can feel it."

Jason looked at the floor. His mother wrapped her arms around him in a hug. "Oh, Jason, it's hard sometimes, isn't it, without your dad around anymore?"

It sounded like she was crying.

Maybe she was the one having a hard time.

Maybe now hadn't been the time to tell her about Sam and Edna. Maybe there never would be a time.

A series of thoughts came into Jason's head:

1. If his mother really found out about Sam and Edna, she might tell school;
2. school might tell the police—
3. or, worse yet, the government and its weird UFO investigators—
4. which meant things would end up like the last scene in the movie *E.T.*,
5. causing heaps of trouble for Sam and Edna the next time they came to Earth, not to mention
6. government guys in hazmat suits and TV crews showing up on Jason's doorstep, with bright lights and cameras, and
7. obnoxious reporters with their slicked-back hair and makeup asking him questions he didn't know the answers to, and
8. doctors poking him to find out if he had some alien disease.

He gently pulled himself out of his mother's hug and looked into her eyes.

"You're right, Mom. There are no aliens. No rocket fuel. It was a science experiment for school that kind of got out of hand. Ms. Rothbar wanted us to make a volcano, a little volcano, just to see what it was like, and I put in too much baking soda and it blew up."

"Why didn't you tell me? I would have helped you."

"You'd gone to bed already."

His mother looked down at her hand. She was still

holding Edna's purple stocking. "Where did this come from? What does a purple stocking have to do with a volcano science experiment?" She had a quizzical expression on her face, as if she was having a hard time putting together the pieces of a strange puzzle.

"Uh, I found it. I liked the color and I thought it could be the wavy purple . . . I mean the blue tropical ocean around the island volcano."

"Oh." His mother glanced at the kitchen clock and abruptly said, "Maybe we should talk about this later. I have to go to work." She put the stocking on the counter and went out the front door.

Jason was left alone in the kitchen.

Sputnik peered in the door. He sniffed, then gingerly started across the kitchen toward his food bowl. Halfway across, he stopped and rocked back and forth on his feet, as if he wanted to be walking but couldn't. He meowed, immobile.

Then it came to Jason: Sputs was stuck to the floor. Adhered to the linoleum.

He started toward the cat but realized that his feet were stuck, too.

Jason looked at Sputnik.

Sputnik looked at Jason.

Jason tried to move his foot. "Ow!"

Sputnik tried to move his feet. "Meooowwwww!"

Jason found that if he twisted himself backward, kind of like one of his mother's yoga postures, he could reach the sink. Stretching his arms out, he turned on the water. He cupped his hands under the faucet, then slowly untwisted, being careful to not spill the water out of his hands. Leaning down, he drizzled it on his feet.

He wiggled his feet. Pulling hard, he managed to free first one foot, then the other. He looked at Sputnik, still rocking back and forth and meowing.

"Poor Sputs." He poured a dribble of water on Sputnik's tiny feet.

Slowly the cat pulled his feet out. He meowed, looking across the room at his food.

Squishsquishsquishsquish—Jason walked across the kitchen and brought him his bowl. Sputnik looked down at the food. After standing a long time over the bowl, he retreated to the living room to lick his feet clean. Jason knew that he should clean up the messy disaster, but if he started in, he would be late for school. The green gunk would have to wait.

Eighteen

*A*s he walked home from school that day, Jason thought about Sam and Edna. It was hard to think of them as aliens. They were not like the strange creatures in science fiction movies, with cold eyes and metallic bodies and nothing but destruction on their minds. They had come from outer space, but they seemed more like grandparents than aliens. Edna even liked Elvis. Still, thought Jason, as he looked at the kitchen, things do have a way of getting out of hand when they show up.

When he opened the kitchen door, a smell of old

broccoli and damp towels hung heavily in the room. The green slime was starting to congeal and turn moldy.

Would the mold eat through the linoleum?

He decided to begin with the floor, filled a bucket with warm water, and started mopping. The gunk made green swirling eddies in the water. Jason liked the rhythm of sloshing the water around. He poured more water onto the floor.

By the time his mother came home, the floor wasn't sticky anymore, but the rest of the kitchen was still what she would call a "certifiable disaster area."

"Ick," she said. She didn't seem to be angry, and without saying much, started helping Jason clean.

He looked at his mother. "Thanks, Mom."

She smiled at him for an instant, but then went back to work.

She was so angry at me this morning, thought Jason. Why not now?

They worked side by side, first cleaning the dishes in the sink, and then his mother scrubbed the stove while Jason cleaned the counters. He could feel that she had something she wanted to say. After a while, she stopped and turned to him.

"Jason, I'm sorry I got mad this morning. I mean, you did make a huge mess in the kitchen, but I know you didn't mean to."

"Sorry, Mom."

"I've been thinking about what happened, and what

you said about aliens, and the purple stocking." She put the sponge down. "I think that if you went to talk to someone about everything, it might make you feel better."

"Someone?"

"Yes, someone who knows about these kinds of things."

"Knows about spaceships and aliens?" This was interesting. Was there someone who might know about aliens like Sam and Edna? "You mean an expert who knows all about real alie—" He stopped himself. "I mean, someone who knows about why kids make things up?"

His mother looked at him. "Yes, someone like that. I talked to a friend and she gave me the number of a man named Dr. Zimburger. He's a therapist, I think, but he also studies UFOs. He's interested in talking to people about aliens."

"A therapist? Isn't that for people who are mental?"

"Mental? Oh, no. Lots of normal people go to talk about their problems."

"Like making things up?"

"Sometimes. People also talk to therapists if they're having trouble in school or something like that. Kind of like a school counselor. You can talk about anything."

Jason looked down at the rag he was holding. "Are you sure you don't think I'm crazy, Mom?"

His mother paused. "No, of course not, Jason. I think

you're a very normal boy with a very, uh, vivid imagination."

Jason looked down at the rag again. His mother didn't think he was crazy. That was a relief. Then suddenly he remembered: Dr. Zimburger! The weird ad on the bus!

"Wait a minute, Mom. Are you sure you didn't find out about Dr. Zimburger on a bus?"

His mother looked away. "Well, yes, actually I did. Or my friend Suzie did."

"Mom, Dr. Zimburger advertises on buses. There's got to be something weird about him. Have you seen the ad? It looks strange to me."

"Suzie said Dr. Zimburger can help people who are worried about aliens. Just try it out, Jason, for my sake. It might help, it really might."

"Help what, Mom?"

"Just try it, honey."

Jason wondered about Dr. Zimburger. Would he be sitting in a wood-paneled office, smoking a pipe? Would he have little hairs that stuck out of his ears or, worse yet, out of his nose? Would Jason have to lie down on a couch and talk about things that made him feel uncomfortable?

Nineteen

A week later, it was time for the visit to the therapist. Jason was going through the pile of magazines in Dr. Zimburger's waiting room, and his mother was next to him, reading *People*. On top of the stack there were regular, boring magazines like *Good Housekeeping* and *Time* and *Vogue*, but at the bottom were other magazines he had never heard of: *Interplanetary Travel World*, *National UFO*, *Galactic Mysteries*. He wriggled out a copy of *Galactic Mysteries*. A headline caught his eye: "Is the Government Holding Alien Hostages in Nevada's Area 51? See page 126."

Jason turned to page 126. At the top of the article was an aerial photo.

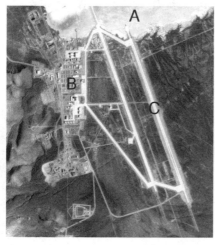

AREA 51

A. Groom Lake

B. Airplane Hangars

C. World's Longest Runway

The article said that Area 51 was in the desert near Groom Lake, Nevada, and was one of the most top-secret U.S. military bases in the country—so secret that it wasn't on any maps. Alien-looking objects had been seen flying over the area at night, but the government would never reveal what they were or why they were flying in such strange ways. It also said that absolutely no airplanes, even military planes, were allowed to fly over the area.

The article quoted Joe Fusterhaus, who used to work as a janitor in Area 51. He said that he had seen alien-looking creatures kept in secret rooms in the basement of one of the hangars. "Yep, seen them with my own eyes. Weird lookin'. Some of them green, some of them blue. Some had big eyes, some little ones. Some of 'em even looked like people."

Jason looked up from the magazine to see a short man with glasses come into the room. A wisp of hair angled across the front of his otherwise bald head, and a neatly trimmed goatee framed his chin. His eyes were intense blue, and his mouth was thin lipped and tight. When he smiled it looked as if something painful was happening to his insides. He smelled like stale cigars.

"Hello, Ms. Jameson. I'm Dr. Zimburger." He spoke with a slight accent. "This young man must be Jason." He shook Jason's hand with a clammy grasp and motioned him into his office.

On one side of the room was a big leather chair, next to it a desk piled high with papers. Behind the desk was a large sign that said

ZIMBOVIA FOREVER

A smaller chair faced the big chair. No couch, thought Jason. That was a good sign. Jason sat down in the small chair. Dr. Zimburger sat in the big chair.

"So, tell me what is going on in your life? Your mother seems a little worried about you."

"Mmmm." Jason was staring at the sign behind the desk. What did "Zimbovia Forever" mean?

"School okay?"

126

"Yeah."

"I understand you had a problem with a science experiment."

"Yeah."

"Something about Gatorade and broccoli and a big mess in the kitchen? You told your mother aliens were involved?"

"Yeah, I mean . . . can I ask you a question?"

"Anything."

"Let's say that all this stuff about aliens really happened to me."

"Yes?"

"Would you tell other people, like reporters and the police and stuff?"

"No. Unless, of course, I felt that someone was in danger. No one seems to be in danger here." The doctor tapped his pencil on his knee. "Let's talk about aliens. Do you like thinking about aliens?"

Duh, thought Jason. Of course I like thinking about Sam and Edna.

"Have you read some books about them?"

"My uncle Miltie gave me *The Giant Atlas of the Universe for Boys and Girls*. That's fun to look at. But it's not about aliens." Jason remembered looking up the Pleiades in Uncle Miltie's book after his trip with Sam.

"Have you ever seen an alien?" The doctor was looking intently at Jason.

Jason was thinking hard. What should he tell Dr.

Zimburger? Should he make stuff up? He knew he would back himself into a corner if he made anything up, so he decided to stick to what happened and trust that it would come out right in the end.

"Yeah, I guess I have. I mean I think so." And Jason described to Dr. Zimburger what had happened to him. The Dart crashing in the empty lot, finding the article in the library, going bongo fishing in the Pleiades, barely escaping the car crusher in San Leandro.

"That's very interesting, very interesting," said the doctor when Jason finished. "What was the name of that magazine again?" He wrote it down in a little notebook. "Now, can you describe the aliens?"

"Well, these aliens weren't green like in the movies, and they didn't have strange eyes or pointy little ears. They looked sort of like regular humans, except they were a little older and had gray-blue hair."

"They sound like someone's grandparents."

"I guess so, except they were small, kind of like midgets."

"Midgets can be grandparents, too, Jason."

"I guess."

"So far you haven't told me anything that makes them different from people on Earth. They sound like ordinary midget grandparents. Was there anything about them that was strange?"

"They were a little blue."

"Blue? Like baby blue? Or deep blue?"

"Baby blue."

"Did the woman alien have a blue tint to her hair? Like some old ladies have blue hair?"

"Yes. And she likes Elvis Presley."

"Elvis, the singer?"

"Yes."

The doctor looked over his glasses and tapped his pencil a little faster on his knee. He smiled at Jason. "Elvis? Really?"

"She wanted to go to Las Vegas to see Elvis."

"Elvis Presley has been dead for many years, Jason."

"I explained that to her, but it didn't seem to matter. She's convinced that he's still alive somewhere in the universe."

The pencil tapped faster on Zimburger's knee. "Okay, so you're telling me that these midget alien grandparents, who look like a retired couple from Florida and love Elvis, came into your kitchen? What were they doing there?"

"Making rocket fuel."

"Rocket fuel? In your kitchen?"

Jason suddenly felt angry with Dr. Zimburger. What did he know about aliens? He sat up in his chair and stared at the doctor. "They had a little silver machine that made rocket fuel. Out of broccoli and some other stuff. It looked kind of like a coffee grinder."

"Kind of like a coffee grinder? A coffee grinder that could make rocket fuel out of broccoli?"

"I think so." Under the doctor's intense stare, Jason

felt less sure of himself. "I mean, whatever it was, it . . . it made the Dart go."

"You've also told me that their spaceship looked like a 1960 Dodge Dart, but I have to say I wonder about that. Why don't we look at some pictures of normal alien spaceships, and you tell me if perhaps their spaceship looked more like one of these."

Dr. Zimburger went to the bookshelf and pulled out a large, leather-bound book. He held the open book up for Jason to look at. "Did their spaceship look like this?"

Jason leaned over to look at the picture. It didn't look like a Dodge Dart at all.

"No."

Dr. Zimburger pointed to another picture. "Like this?"

"No."

He turned the page. There were lots of pictures of strange-looking UFOs on it.

"Here, why don't you look at the book a little more closely?" Dr. Zimburger handed it to Jason. Jason held the book in his lap and looked at the pictures. None of them looked like a Dodge Dart. He turned the page. Even more strange-looking UFO pictures.

"No, it's not here." Jason felt mad again. "It really did look just like a 1960 Dodge Dart."

"Heh . . . heh . . . I mean, uh, this is quite interesting." The doctor put the tips of his fingers together and looked up at the ceiling. "Aliens who look like someone's midget grandparents, drive a lime-green Dodge Dart around the universe, and have a liking for Elvis Presley? Quite marvelous, Jason. Quite a terrific imagination."

Jason felt pride at his creative imagination rising in his mind. Then he caught himself. Sam and Edna were as real as his own hand, and his "terrific imagination" hadn't created anything. Couldn't Dr. Zimburger see that Sam and Edna were real? He had been afraid Dr. Zimburger would reveal his secret, and now he wanted to stand up and shout, "They're real! As real as chewing gum! As real as hot dogs!"

Dr. Zimburger went to the door and asked Jason's mother to come in.

"So, Ms. Jameson, you have a fine son here, a smart boy, and very high-functioning in the imagination department. A very creative mind."

Jason's mother smiled. Dr. Zimburger smiled. He took out a handkerchief and wiped the beads of sweat off his upper lip. "He just needs an outlet for his wonderful imagination. I would encourage him to write down his stories and read science fiction writers, like Arthur C. Clarke or Isaac Asimov. Jason might have the potential to write science fiction someday." Dr. Zimburger smiled again and laughed a hollow-sounding laugh. "Next thing you know, he'll tell me they had a ray gun. Haha. That would be funny." But there was something in his voice that sounded as if he didn't think it was funny at all, and his eyes narrowed to dark slits as he said it.

Jason thought, If only Dr. Zimburger knew what it's like to fly across the universe with an alien from the Pleiades in a 1960 Dodge Dart, to watch bongo fish flying through the air in Zorcovado Planet Park, to see the dark side of the moon. Dr. Zimburger has no idea, no idea at all.

Jason's mother smiled at the doctor. "Aliens wouldn't wear purple stockings, would they?"

The doctor laughed that laugh.

Just then a tall, powerfully built man with short-cropped dark hair and a long mustache came into the waiting room from the street. Jason noticed that he had blue eyes of the same intensity as Dr. Zimburger. He smiled at Jason and his mother, showing a gold tooth. Jason thought he looked like the bad guy, Oddjob, in *Goldfinger*. The big man brushed past Dr. Zimburger and went directly into his office, and Jason thought he saw the doctor whisper something to the big man and point to Jason as he shut the door behind them.

As Jason and his mother walked back to the car he said, "Who was that big guy?"

"Well, I'm sure he was one of Dr. Zimburger's patients, dear."

But Oddjob didn't look like a patient to Jason. More like a large toad with a mustache and an attitude.

Twenty

*D*uring the next week things started to get mysterious:

1. Sputnik got sick and threw up and got blue spots on his belly. When they took him to the Solano Pet Hospital, the vet said he had never seen blue spots on a cat's belly and he had no idea what to do. He charged Jason's mother fifty-six dollars for the visit.

2. Jason got an A on his history exam. That had never happened before.

3. A small black car started parking across the street from Jason's apartment. It had tinted windows and a futuristic-looking antenna that rotated slowly around and around, and someone was always sitting inside, but Jason could never see who. Whenever Jason walked near it, the black car drove away.

4. When the black car was parked near Jason's house, there was a lot of static on the radio in Jason's bedroom.

5. Jason went to the library to do a little sleuthing, and Marge the librarian told him that, yes, someone else *had* come looking for *Automotive Mystery World,* and yes, the man had a beard and smelled like cigars.

6. Jason looked up Zimbovia on Wikipedia. Hidden high in the mountains between Bulgaria and Romania, it had been a tiny country whose king was Zambo VI. He believed that his people were descended from a race of superior alien UFO invaders, and he rode around in a car that looked like a space saucer. In 1982, when the king died of apoplexy, leaving no heir, the Bulgarians had invaded Zimbovia, and it no longer existed. But his space car was displayed in the Bulgarian National Museum.

   The Wikipedia article also gave the website address for the Society for the Preservation of Zimbovian

Culture, but you needed a password to get in. The motto at the top of the page said *Zimbovia Forever*, and at the bottom it said *Zimbovia Will Rise Again!*

7. After school one day, as Jason was walking toward the empty lot on Ninth Street, he saw a man behind the piles of dirt at the back, taking photos of the ground and sweeping a metal detector over the spot where the Dart had landed. Jason walked as casually as he could past the empty lot, glancing from under his baseball cap at the man. Who was he? What was he doing there? Why was he so interested in that particular spot? The man turned to give Jason a hard stare. Suddenly whistling an aimless tune, Jason walked away as fast as he could. He turned to look back from the end of the block and saw the man driving away in a black car.

Although Jason told his mother some of the things on his mystery list, she just patted his head and said, "I'm sure there must be a simple explanation, Jason. I wouldn't worry about it. And I'm sure Sputnik will get better soon." Then she went back to her yoga.

Twenty-One

*B*ut Jason *was* worried. That night after dinner, he opened his top drawer and pulled out the business card that Sam had given him. The long number on the bottom looked like a phone number, a really long phone number.

Jason counted twenty-five digits in the number altogether, if you included the one at the beginning.

Well, I could give it a try, he thought to himself. Then again, how could I call the Pleiades? That's a ridiculous idea. But on the other hand . . .

He waited until his mother had gone to bed, tiptoed into the kitchen, and picked up the phone. Carefully he started dialing the numbers on the card: "One, four, two, six . . ." until he had dialed all twenty-five.

A high-pitched recorded voice came on the line. "Please dial more carefully." The line went dead.

How would an operator on Earth know how to call another world? thought Jason. Then again, maybe it would work if he dialed zero first. He tried it that way.

Again the high-pitched voice: "If you are trying to contact another universe, do not dial four, two, six. You must dial four hundred and twenty-six *ones BEFORE* you dial eight, zero, zero."

Jason looked at the phone. Four hundred twenty-six ones? How long would that take? He started pushing the one button on the phone and counting: "One, two, three, four, five . . ." On and on he went.

Sputnik wandered through the door and climbed onto his lap.

Poor Sputs, thought Jason, looking at the blue spots on his belly, and in that instant he forgot. Was he on 391 or 392?

"Rats." He kept on, until he thought he'd come to 426. Then the rest of the numbers.

Again the voice on the phone: "You must dial exactly four hundred and twenty-six ones, not four hundred and twenty-five. Please dial better. Have a very pleasant day."

He put Sputs on the floor and tried dialing again. When he finished, he pressed the phone to his ear. Far away he heard *click . . . click . . . click.* Then a series of beeps and whistles. Then . . . a phone ringing! Jason's heart leaped, and he imagined Sam reaching for the receiver in a cozy little house in the Pleiades.

The ringing stopped.

Again the screechy voice: "I'm sorry. All intergalactic circuits are busy. Please try your call another time, in an eon or two. Have a pleasant day." *Click.*

Maybe it was a joke anyway, thought Jason, some computer nerd's way of having fun. He picked up Sputnik and walked back to his room.

Of course you can't call another universe, he thought. It's too far away.

"How is the patient today?" asked Jason's mother a few days later at dinner.

Jason looked down at Sputnik in his lap.

"About the same."

"Maybe it's cat measles."

"Blue measles? I don't think so." Jason picked up Sputnik and carried him to his room. "It's okay, Sputsy, everything is going to be okay."

He sat on the bed. What was that disease that people got? Cancer? Did cats get diabetes? Sputnik sneezed. Were blue spots life-threatening? What did that mean, anyway, life-threatening? Was a meteor life-threatening? Appendicitis? He felt Sputnik's body. Did he have any strange bumps?

Jason rummaged through the socks and underwear in his top drawer. Where was that Confabulator thing Edna had given him? Maybe it could locate Sam and Edna. At the back he felt its cool metal shape, about the size of a package of Junior Mints. He pulled it out and turned it over in his hands. In the middle was a glass panel, behind it a bright red button. It was like the alarm boxes at school—the ones that said BREAK GLASS IN CASE OF FIRE.

Jason wondered how such a tiny box could send a signal four hundred light-years away, but then again, weird things were going on and he might as well try it.

He climbed out the window and down the stairs into the backyard. By the light from Mrs. Sherbatskoy's window he found a small rock and broke the glass pane on the Confabulator. The red button inside began to glow rhythmically, and the box hummed with electricity as a long antenna slid out the top. He held the Confabulator in front of him, pointed the antenna straight up, and pushed the button.

The box buzzed wildly in his hands and then: *CRACK!* A bright blue light shot out of the antenna, throwing Jason to the ground as it sizzled and whipped off into the distance like a bolt of lightning. He watched the light soar into the night like a neon-bright firework, growing fainter as it traveled outward and then receding into nothingness in the eastern sky.

Sitting dazed on the ground, Jason heard a voice behind him. "Kids these days."

He turned to see Mrs. Sherbatskoy staring down from her back porch, shaking her corpulent finger at him. "You watch out with that thing, young man. That toy could hurt someone."

Toy? thought Jason. Toy?

He climbed up the stairs and through the window, and curled up next to Sputnik on the bed. Soon they were fast asleep.

The next day, and for days afterward, Jason ran home from school, hoping to find a note on his dresser from Sam and Edna or the sound of snoring coming from his closet. But each day there was nothing. And Sputnik wasn't getting any better. There were more blue spots on his belly, and he was sweaty and slept a lot. The mysterious black car still hung around in front of the apartment, always with its tinted windows up, sometimes with its little roof antenna rotating slowly. But where were Sam and Edna?

With no word by the end of the week, Jason decided that the Confabulator was nothing more than a good light show, useless fireworks for a hopeless cause.

I guess that's that, he thought as he climbed into bed. Staring up at the ceiling, he wondered if he would ever see Sam and Edna again. Maybe they had gone on to other galaxies, other worlds, other friends. Jason felt smaller than small in a bigger than big universe.

Twenty-Two

While Jason and Sputnik slept, a cold fog began to swirl through Berkeley, curling around the streetlights on San Pablo Avenue, slipping down Shattuck, licking at the hills. From above the fog, the lights of the city glowed softly, as if through a layer of cotton. To the west the two towers of the Golden Gate Bridge poked up like orange bedposts above a white quilt. The moon shone down from a deep black sky, and to the south the lights of airplanes twinkled as they headed toward the Oakland airport. The sky above Berkeley seemed empty of moving things, but if you could have looked out into the night, far above the Earth, above the atmosphere and a little to the left of the moon, you would have seen a small light shining through the darkness, speeding straight down toward the city. The light occasionally wobbled as it went, but it always regained its direction and sped resolutely on. If you had looked closely at it, you would have seen that the light was a headlight attached to a sleek metal object tearing through the atmosphere, an object shaped like a motorcycle but surrounded by a teardrop shell of aluminum, once shiny, now rusty and dented. Every so often, flames shot out of the tailpipe, and at other times, black smoke. Looking in through the windshield as the object sped through space, you would have seen, lit by glowing dials, a deeply absorbed figure, staring alternately at the dials and then intently down at the Earth growing larger below. Onward sped the machine, down toward Berkeley, trying to keep itself on course.

At home in bed, Jason mumbled in his sleep, shifted his body, then settled on his back and was again in a deep slumber. Sputnik sighed a tiny cat sigh and snuggled closer to Jason.

Taptap . . . taptap, a sound made its way into Jason's sleeping brain. He drifted up to consciousness, his mind foggy. The *taptap* stopped for a moment and then insistently started again. Sputnik meowed and Jason reached out to soothe him, but then the tapping started again.

He sat up and looked around the room, eyes half open. Where was the sound coming from? The closet? The door? He turned toward the window.

"Edna!" he exclaimed. Her nose was flattened against the pane. She waved at Jason.

He pulled up the window and she tumbled in, dragging her purse behind her. Dressed in a leather jacket and boots, she was breathing heavily, her face grimy with soot. She unwrapped a pink scarf from her neck, pulled off a pair of leather gloves, and looked around the room. "This place is a mess, kid. Look at those socks." She sat down at the edge of the bed and brushed a strand of blue hair out of her eyes. "Got a drink of water?" Jason beamed at her. At last she had come. The confabulator had worked.

He snuck to the kitchen and came back with a glass of water and a chocolate chip cookie.

"So, what's up?" she asked, munching loudly.

"Sputs is sick. And weird stuff is happening."

"Like what?"

Sitting next to Edna on the bed, Jason told her every-thing that had happened since the visit to Dr. Zim-burger. When he finished, Edna sat quietly thinking. Then she wiggled her finger in her ear. "Ooh, that rocket cycle is loud. What do you think that doctor guy wants with a UFO? I mean, *our* UFO?"

Jason shrugged his shoulders.

"Sounds like a detective story to me," said Edna. "I love mysteries, I read them all the time."

She picked up Sputnik. "Look at those spots. If you ask me, he's got bleazles."

"Bleazles?"

"Yeah, Pleiades blue measles. Bleazles." She looked at Jason again. "So Zimbooger, or whatever his name is, pretends not to believe you, then he shows up at the library looking for that magazine. But who was that other guy at the empty lot? And what about the black car?"

"It's still here. At least I think so." Jason and Edna tiptoed into the living room and Jason pulled aside the curtains. Far down the street he could just make out the black car.

"There."

As they watched, its headlights came on and it slowly drove past the apartment, antenna revolving. Jason and Edna went back to his room. She had a grim look on her face as she picked Sputnik up again. "The germs must have come with us in the Dart. Come to think of it, my cousin Betty's cat Poof had the bleazles a month ago. But Sputnik's got a temperature too. He doesn't look so good. So where's Sam? Is he asleep in the closet or something?"

"Sam?"

"He's not here? You're kidding. He left a couple of days ago. When we got the Confabulator message, he said he was going straight to Earth. Then he didn't come home for dinner and I got lonely. I came down here to join the party."

"Maybe he got lost."

"Sam? Never. Problem is, we're a one-spaceship family. I keep telling Sam he should sell those junkers behind the garage and get me a nice little baby-blue spaceship I can visit my mother in. But no, Sam likes his junkers. So I got nothing to fly to Earth in except the old rocket cycle. He keeps it under a tarp in the garage. Didn't look too great, but somehow I got it started. Steering's a little loose, but the air lock's okay, levitators work, and it had gas and some antigas too. I grabbed the maps and took off."

"Does it go as fast as the Dart?"

"Pretty fair clip. Maybe nine, ten times light speed on a good day. Took a while to get straightened out after I took a wrong turn at Orion and missed the wormhole by Centaurus, but then I circled back. It's hard to miss Earth: such a beautiful planet."

She stood up abruptly and started pulling her gloves on. "We got to find Sam. That's the main thing. Then we can deal with the cat and that weird doctor. I got a funny feeling about him." She started toward the window. "How big is the Earth anyway?"

"Pretty big."

"I bet we can see where Sam is on the rocket cycle screen," said Edna. "I don't know exactly how it works, but you're a smart kid. I think you can figure it out."

Twenty-Three

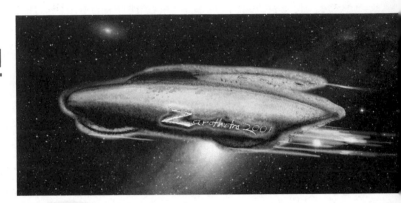

Jason hugged Sputnik. "You have to stay here, Sputs. We'll be back soon." Sputnik stared up at him as he turned and climbed out the window. He stood on the fire escape looking up at the vast dome of the night sky.

When *would* they be back? How could they find Sam? He could be anywhere in the big lonely universe. He looked down. Floating in the air next to the railing was a silver, bullet-shaped machine. Though rusty in places its metallic skin glimmered in the darkness, and it hummed slightly as it rocked back and forth, engine chugging, dials glowing through the windshield. It was like a sleekly powerful animal, a cheetah or a racehorse, restless and eager to run.

On the side, large letters read ZARATHUSTRA 2001. A row of winking green lights ran from the nose to the tail, and wisps of smoke drifted up from the exhaust pipe. A chain held the cycle to the railing, and a bright purple lock with a digital dial ticked off the seconds.

"Didn't want anyone to run off with it," said Edna. She slid the hatch open and Jason peered inside. The metal cockpit was small and cramped, with a musty smell, and the seat had rips in it and pieces of stuffing falling out. A few loose wires stuck out of the dials on the front, but at the same time the dials seemed energized and complex and powerful, and there were lots of them crammed into the small space at the front of the cycle. As the engine chugged and rumbled, the dials moved up and down, glowing alternately softer and brighter. In the middle of them was a TV screen with a map on it and a glowing blip in the middle.

"It's Berkeley," said Jason, pointing. He could see his street on the map, and the glowing blip was right over his house. "It's like a GPS."

"What's a GPS?" asked Edna.

"It's kind of like a map, but you can see it on a computer screen."

"Will it tell us where Sam is?"

"You're asking me?"

"I never used it on Earth before."

Jason knelt down and looked more closely at the screen, Edna peering over his shoulder.

Meanwhile, Sputnik raised himself feebly and looked out the window. He tottered tentatively out onto the fire escape, as if wondering what to do, but as if also afraid to stay behind without Jason. He looked up at Jason and Edna engrossed in the rocket cycle, then sniffed at Edna's purse, which was sitting next to the cycle. He pawed at it, tipping it over, and before Jason or Edna noticed, he climbed in. After a sneeze that was muffled by the purse, he curled up and went to sleep.

Meanwhile, Jason was studying the screen on the rocket cycle. Across the top was a series of tiny icons. He started to touch them, one by one.

Some didn't change the screen at all, but others gave different views, maps with alien writing all over them. He came to the last icon, a small blue and green circle. As he touched it, the screen changed again. Now it was a map with English writing on it. In the middle was a bright blue dot that blinked on and off, and at the top of the screen were the letters POV-SAM.

Edna looked at the screen. "POV-SAM. That's Sam, that's the Dart! I know it."

"POV? What does that mean?"

"It means Pleiades Operating Vehicle. You know, it's like a radio-wave license plate." Jason leaned closer. At first it was hard to orient himself, but then, with a start, he recognized the map: It looked like the map in the UFO magazine in Dr. Zimburger's office.

"Sam's in Nevada!"

"Isn't that where Las Vegas is? Always wanted to go to Las Vegas."

"Yeah, but he isn't in Las Vegas. He's somewhere near Area 51!"

"Area 51? Weird name for a town."

"No, it's not a town, it's this place where, it's hard to explain, but we . . . WE SHOULD GET GOING." Jason's mind was racing. "It's a big secret government place where they fly mysterious airplanes and study aliens. Sometimes the government finds out where UFOs have crashed on Earth, and they go and catch the aliens and take them back to Area 51 to study them."

"What?" Edna looked at Jason with alarm. "They poke little things in them, like doctors? Sam hates doctors."

Jason nodded. "Will the rocket cycle take two of us?"

"You got a helmet?"

Jason climbed back through the window and soon emerged, wearing a black sweatshirt, black pants, and his bicycle helmet.

"Looks cute," said Edna, straightening it on his head. "Now we have to take the top off the cycle." Edna pulled a wrench out of her purse and quickly unscrewed two bolts, one on either side of the cycle. "Not so stuffy with the top off, and we can look for Sam easier." They balanced the top on the fire escape.

It teetered there for a moment and then crashed into the yard below. A dog barked in the neighbor's yard, and Jason could see Mrs. Sherbatskoy trying to peer out her kitchen window. Edna shrugged and climbed onto the cycle. Jason squeezed himself behind her. She reached out, unlocked the chain and tucked it into her purse, then zipped the bag up and held it out for Jason. "Can you hold this? Thing gets heavier all the time."

"Doesn't surprise me," said Jason as he slipped the straps over his shoulder, remembering all the things he'd seen come out of the purse when they were making rocket fuel.

It does seem heavy, he thought. And kind of wiggly. But you never knew what might be inside Edna's purse. She began flipping a series of switches on the dashboard, then hesitated. "Now, which one? This one . . . or . . . let's try this one." Jason thought he heard something like a cat sneeze, but just as he turned to look in the bedroom, Edna pushed a large red button.

BLAM!

With a jolt, the cycle sprang forward, jerking them back. Jason locked his arms around Edna.

The machine roared away from the building, straight at Mrs. Sherbatskoy washing dishes in her kitchen. Jason gasped, but at the last second, Edna pulled up on the handlebars and they climbed into the fog, engine full on, flames shooting out the back. Helmet askew, he clutched Edna tightly.

"Could you ease up a bit, kid? I can't breathe."

Jason opened his mouth to say something, but the sound of the engine drowned him out.

Soon they burst out of the fog and into the clear night sky. The moon was above, fog below, the city hidden in a blanket of white.

"Pretty nice, huh?" Edna yelled, waving her arm at the night sky above them.

"It's like, like . . ." Jason couldn't think of anything to say.

"Which way do we go?" asked Edna.

"Doesn't the screen show the way?"

"Tells me where Sam is, but not how to get there. Or maybe it does, but I always forget which button is which."

Jason looked down at the fog. At first he was disoriented, then he saw the Berkeley hills rising out of the mist away to the left. He knew that the hills were the eastern side of Berkeley, and Nevada was east of California, so that was the way to go, over the hills and out across the Central Valley. Then they would have to go over the high mountains, the Sierra Nevadas.

"That way," he said, pointing toward the hills.

Edna twisted the accelerator handle and turned the rocket cycle east. The machine sped upward, the wind blowing in Jason's face. They leaped over the ridge of the Berkeley hills and out into the suburbs, the fog now gone, rolling hills and endless rows of suburban houses stretching into the distance. Below, he could see the houses and streetlights of Orinda and Walnut Creek. Off to the left was Mount Diablo. Already they were far above the mountain. Jason looked down.

"Does it have seat belts?" he yelled to Edna.

"Seal pelts?"

"No, SEAT BELTS!"

"Oh, seat belts. Let me take a look!" She twisted around, but as she turned, the handlebars twisted also, rotating the cycle down. Edna seemed not to notice, as she muttered to herself and fumbled for the seat belts.

"Watch out!" cried Jason. The cycle was flying on its side, and he was hanging into empty space, his grip on the purse slipping.

"Sorry about that!" she yelled as she pulled the cycle upright. Jason pulled the purse in. What did Edna have in it? A bowling ball?

"Forget about the seat belts! It's safer not to look for them." Off to the right were the giant turbines of the Altamont wind farm, hundreds of them spread out over the open hills, their huge propellers spinning in the night. The rocket cycle soared past the windmills and out over the Central Valley.

Below, Jason could see the lights of towns, dark rectangular shapes of fields, and moonlit irrigation canals. In the distance loomed the high mountains of the Sierras.

"Button up your overcoat," yelled Edna.

"I haven't got one."

"Then snuggle up, kid. It's going to get chilly."

The cycle rose farther up into the night. As they flew into the mountains and away from the towns of the Central Valley, the lights were sparser. The land below was dark, forested. Jason's fingers were cold, and the wind whipped against his pant legs. He nestled his head against Edna's back to get out of the wind. Feeling the warmth of her body under her coat, he wondered, Do Sam and Edna have hearts like ours? Do they feel things the way I do? Surely they do, but they are from so far away, from across the universe and yet somehow so near. Jason smiled to himself. They really are ordinary midget grandparents.

In the distance Jason could see the sweep of the mountains, the high ridges of the Sierras glowing softly in the moonlight.

"It's so beautiful!" said Edna.

"Where are we?" asked Jason, looking around.

She looked at the screen in front of her. "I can see the Dart on this map, but I can't see *us*. Screen keeps flickering on and off. Maybe Earth gravity interferes with it."

Jason looked down at the mountains. They all looked the same in the moonlight. Then he looked behind. In the distance he saw the blinking red and green lights of an airplane.

"Don't look now, but I think there's someone following us," he yelled to Edna.

"Where?" She turned the rocket cycle hard to the right, straining to see behind them.

Jason once more lost his grip. "GAAAAAAAAH!" He leaned out over empty space, clutching nothing, the wind hard in his face, his foot twisted on the footrest. Edna's purse again slipped down his arm.

"I see them," cried Edna.

Jason slowly pulled himself up. "Ooooooh." He let out a long breath. His hands were numb, his arms shaking. "What'll we do?"

"I'll cut the running lights and put up the radar shield. We need to find a place to hunker down." She flipped a row of switches and pushed down on the handlebars. They began to descend toward the forest, losing altitude quickly.

"Watch out for the trees!" cried Jason.

The cycle seemed to be going faster, not slower, as it descended. Jason closed his eyes and gripped tighter around Edna's waist as they roared straight down.

Abruptly the cycle slowed and came almost to a stop. He opened his eyes. They were floating among the trees. The dark forest stretched out in front of them.

"How do you like that, kid? At least I know how to slow this thing down."

The rocket cycle drifted gently down into the forest, pine branches brushing against Jason's legs.

"Any place to land?" Edna leaned out and looked down.

"Too many trees," said Jason.

"We'll have to hold steady here in the branches."

Soon the plane flew overhead. It was a small plane with a single engine, perhaps painted black. It circled twice, slowly. Looking through the branches overhead, Jason could see someone leaning out of the plane with a pair of binoculars, scanning the forest. After making another circle, it flew off. They waited for the plane to come back, but the sound disappeared in the distance.

"Got rid of them," said Edna. "Now let's find a place to land and stretch the legs." They rose above the trees, looking for any sign of the plane.

"We can fly without the running lights, but I'll have to take the radar shield off," said Edna. "The locator won't work with it on."

They pressed on.

"Look over there." Jason pointed.

Edna turned the cycle. "It's a lake."

"Maybe it has a beach we can land on."

"Okay, slow it down. . . . Come on in real easy." Edna was talking to herself. "Number one: Turn on the landing lights."

A ring of yellow lights encircled the rocket cycle, and a bright light shone down to the ground.

Edna slowed down even more, until they were barely moving, floating above the trees and gently gliding toward the lake. The cycle was quiet, lights shining into the trees near the water.

*B*elow the rocket cycle, in the woods near the edge of the lake, it happened that Harold Fizzbo, his wife, Doris, and their two children, Amber and Chelsee, were snuggling into their sleeping bags in their E-Z Camp tent. They had driven all the way from Normal, Oklahoma, in their behemoth SUV on this, their first camping trip, their first night in the wilds of California. They had found their campsite at Lower Chickadee Lake, and after a dinner of slightly charred macaroni and cheese they had watched the sun go down over the peaceful lake, until the mosquitoes came out and buzzed around their heads and stung Amber and Chelsee on their pudgy little arms.

Now at last they were safe in their sleeping bags.

"Good night, Amber."

"Good night, Mom."

"Good night, Dad."

Slap! "OW!" Mr. Fizzbo had missed the mosquito that was buzzing next to his ear. "Good night, Chelsee."

Slap!

Soon the mosquitoes settled down, and the Fizzbo family, tucked into their sleeping bags in their cozy tent, closed their eyes.

Just then, the rocket cycle glided directly above them, its landing light shining down.

Mr. Fizzbo opened his eyes. "Doris, did you see that?"

Doris's eyes were wide open. "Y . . . y . . . es. . . ."

Mr. Fizzbo climbed out of his sleeping bag, unzipped the tent, and stepped outside in his pajamas. The night air was cool, and the wind rustled in the pines. Pinecones prickled his feet. Mr. Fizzbo looked all around. He leaned back into the tent. "Everything normal." Then, through the trees, Mr. Fizzbo saw the light again. It was circling, silently.

"Honey, you should take a look at this," he whispered.

"Do I have to?"

Mr. Fizzbo felt at that moment afraid and alone, so he said, "Yes, dear." Mrs. Fizzbo climbed out of the tent and stood in her pink nightgown, clutching her husband. "Oh!" she cried as she saw the light circling lower and lower. The Fizzbos stood rooted to the ground, eyes wide, hearts pounding.

Edna maneuvered the rocket cycle down toward the beach, finally touching the sand with a gentle bump. She left the lights on, and Jason climbed stiffly off the cycle, putting Edna's purse on the beach. He walked around the cycle, stretching his legs and trying to straighten his arms. As he was extending his arms out in front of him, he walked in front of the headlight of the cycle.

If you had been standing where the Fizzbos were standing, next to their tent, you would have seen a small being with something shiny and dark on his head (Jason's bike helmet), arms outstretched ominously, walking toward you.

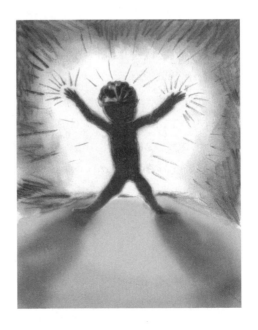

"GAAAH!" said Mrs. Fizzbo.

"GAAAAAAAH!" said Mr. Fizzbo.

Plainly this must be a UFO, and one of the creatures that came out of it was coming toward them, perhaps to kidnap them or demolish them with a laser blast. They had heard that strange things happen in California, but this was more than their brains could handle. Harold clutched his wife's hand and inched toward the tent flap, wishing they had stayed home.

"Girls! Get up! Quick!" he whispered loudly.

Amber and Chelsee sleepily appeared. Their parents grabbed them and ran toward their SUV. They piled into the car pell-mell, falling over one another. Mr. Fizzbo frantically started the engine and jammed the giant car in reverse, smashing its rear bumper into a pine tree. Then he slammed it into drive, gunning the engine, and smashed into another tree in front. Again he jammed the car into reverse, then again into forward, and roared out of the campsite, back down the mountain, tires squealing. The SUV careened along Highway 50, down to the Central Valley, and screeched to a stop at a Motel 6. There the Fizzbo family spent the night, eyes wide open, teeth chattering. The next day they drove straight home to their gated community in Normal, Oklahoma, and they never, ever went to California again.

Twenty-Five

*E*dna and Jason stood staring at the lights of the SUV as it roared down the mountain.

"Who was that?" said Jason.

"Guy doesn't know how to drive. Poor trees," said Edna. "Look at all the stuff they left."

"They must have thought we were aliens!" said Jason, laughing.

"We *are* aliens. . . . At least I am."

"Yeah, but not *that* kind of alien. I mean, you like Elvis. You're like somebody's grandmother."

"Right," said Edna, "a grandmother who descends from the Pleiades on a rocket cycle."

A camp stove stood on the picnic table next to a propane lantern. A sleeping bag lay halfway out of the tent.

Jason picked up a half-eaten bag of potato chips and two bottles of water from under the picnic table. "I guess this stuff is ours now."

"One bottle for us, and one for Sam," said Edna. "Just in case."

They sat on the beach in the moonlight, passing the bag of potato chips and the bottle of water back and forth, as tiny waves broke on the sand.

Edna looked up at the sky. "It's funny, you know, whatever planet Sam's on, we always seem to find each other. Sometimes I can feel it in my bones."

Jason patted her on the back. "We'll find him, I know we will."

They sat in silence on the sand.

"Meow."

"Did those people forget their cat?" said Jason, looking around the campsite. Edna's purse, which they had forgotten next to the rocket cycle, tipped over.

"Achoo!"

Jason looked at Edna. "What did you put in your purse now?"

Edna shrugged her shoulders.

"Achoo!"

Jason tiptoed toward the purse and opened the latch.

Slowly and with unsteady legs, a ball of fur crept out of the purse, stumbled a few steps, and threw up on Jason's shoe.

"Sputnik!"

Sputnik sneezed.

"Sputs!" Jason hugged the cat to him, forgetting the mess on his shoe. How close he had come to dropping Edna's purse when they were in the air! He rocked back and forth with the cat in his arms, then took Sputnik to the edge of the lake, washed him off, and washed the stuff off his shoe, while Sputnik lapped at the water.

"I told you that cat liked my purse," said Edna.

Jason picked up Sputnik again. "Just couldn't stay home, could you? Sputsy never wants to miss a thing."

Edna reached out her hand to the cat. "He's even hotter than when we left."

Jason stroked Sputnik's damp fur.

Edna found a paper towel by the picnic table, dunked it in the lake, and used it to cool off the cat. Then she went back to the lake and splashed the cool lake water on her face. "Time to hit the road."

Jason stuffed the remaining bottle of water into his sweatshirt pocket and they climbed back on.

"Gonna put the cat back in the purse?"

But Sputnik yowled loudly when faced with the purse. Jason gently picked him up and zipped him into his sweatshirt so that only his head stuck out.

Sputnik purred contentedly, as if to say, "That's better."

As Edna was about to start the cycle, they heard the sound of a small plane droning in the distance. Slowly it grew louder.

"Get the rocket cycle under the trees, quick," said Edna. Soon they could see the plane above them through the branches.

"Is it the same one?" whispered Edna.

"I think so."

The plane's wings glinted in the moonlight as it circled the lake slowly. It swooped down toward the beach as if to land. Jason held his breath, his heart pounding. The plane seemed close enough to touch. At the end of the beach it banked away steeply and circled once more, then flew off to the south. Jason and Edna waited a long time, then came out from under the tree.

"I don't like those guys, whoever they are," said Edna. "Let's get out of here."

They taxied down the beach and out over the water, then quickly rose higher into the sky.

"Meow." Sputnik's watery eyes opened wide.

Now there were no lights below, no forest, only the vast rocky peaks of the Sierras above the tree line. Snow, glistening and sharp, was tucked into the folds of the big peaks. The mountains were magnificent in the moonlight, a great parade of rocky shapes from north to south. Jason watched them pass beneath, spellbound.

"Look!" cried Edna.

The mountains fell away; they were past the high

peaks and out into the desert, feeling the warm air rise to meet them. In the distance, Jason saw a lake. Was that Mono Lake? He had heard of it but never seen it. Was it near Area 51? He couldn't remember. What did Area 51 look like? Would there be a big fence around it? Lots of lights and black jets furtively guarding it? Or no lights at all, since it was top secret? He looked down at the land beneath, empty and desolate. Nervously he looked over his shoulder. But the sky was empty.

Jason felt tense. The strange plane following them was gone for the moment, but who knew what lay ahead? Were they heading toward a trap? If they were captured in Area 51, would the government investigators think he was an alien, too? Would he have to lie under bright lights while they poked him and gave him weird tests? Would they let him call his mother? Would anyone believe he wasn't an alien?

He decided that if he was captured by secret government agents, he would:

1. Speak English.
2. Show them that his skin wasn't blue, and he didn't have pointed ears.
3. Tell them that he was born in Alta Bates Hospital, in Berkeley, California, and give them his birth date.

But what about Sam and Edna? What would they do? The more Jason tried to figure it out, the more impossible it seemed and the more tired he grew, until his thoughts became a confused jumble and his eyelids began to droop.

He leaned his head against Edna's back, and soon he was fast asleep, breathing quietly, arms locked around her waist, the purse flapping behind him, endless desert rolling by below. Sputnik's eyes closed too, his feverish body against Jason's chest. On flew the cycle, into the emptiness of Nevada.

"Gettin' close!" Jason was awakened by the sound of Edna's voice.

He looked around sleepily. The same moon, the same desert, the same empty view all the way to the horizon. His arms were starting to ache again.

Edna pointed. "Look. The sky is brighter ahead. Maybe that's Area 62."

"Area 51! Fly lower. Can you put up the radar shield?"

"Can't do that," said Edna. "We wouldn't be able to track Sam. Got to take *evasive action*."

She swung the cycle down toward the desert, at first turning the handlebars back and forth gently, then more boldly, twisting up and down in a series of mad dives and spirals. One minute they were flying upside down, the next sideways, the next seemingly backward. The potato chips in Jason's stomach began to rebel, and Sputnik began to yowl. As the rocket cycle careened wildly, the water bottle in Jason's pocket slithered out and tumbled to the ground far below.

"I feel like I'm gonna throw up," he yelled to Edna. "Sorry."

"Just fly close to the ground. I think that's the way to evade airplane radar."

Edna swooped the rocket cycle toward the desert floor. Now they were flying just above rocky hills and giant boulders. The land rose higher, and behind a far hill they could see the glow of lights. A large sign passed below them:

WARNING: RESTRICTED AREA.
NO ENTRY. USE OF FORCE AUTHORIZED.

They cleared the top of the hill and were looking down a long, bleak valley. There, miles away, glowed the dim outlines of an enormous runway, and next to it huge hangars and concrete buildings. There were no planes on the runway, but a few ominous-looking black helicopters crouched next to the hangars.

"Is this the place you were talking about, kid?"

"I think so. It looks like the photo of Area 51 I saw in that magazine."

"How are we ever going to find Sam in all those buildings?" said Edna.

"We'll just have to look around. You said you could sense where Sam is. Do you feel like he's close by?"

Edna shook her head. "I don't, that's the thing." She looked down at the screen. "Wait! That POV dot's in a

169

different place now. It's not down in that valley, it's off toward those hills there." Edna pointed to the left. "Sam's somewhere over there!"

"Really?" Jason strained to see the screen over her shoulder. "He's not in Area 51 after all?"

"Doesn't look like it, kid."

Jason laughed. No Area 51! What a relief!

Then he looked back down the valley. A siren went off, and lights came on around the buildings. Instantly the runway was lit as bright as day, and the black helicopters churned to life.

People in uniforms were running toward the helicopters.

"Uh-oh."

"They saw us?"

Jason nodded.

"Let's get out of here."

Edna gunned the cycle, and they turned east. Jason looked back as one of the helicopters took off.

"Can you go faster?"

"I've got it at top Earth speed, kid."

They looked out at the land in front of them: hill after hill dotted with sagebrush and nothing else. No place to hide.

Edna leaned forward into the wind as if she was trying to make the cycle go faster. They passed over another ridge. Again, nothing but empty hills and sagebrush. Jason looked down. "There, a tree!"

Edna tilted the machine down toward the gnarled desert pine below them, all by itself in a dry creek bed. The thumping sound of the helicopter drew nearer. How could a helicopter fly so fast? Jason wondered. Edna cut the engine and the cycle landed on its nose, balanced for a second as if it was going to tip over headfirst, and then flopped on its side. Jason and Edna and Sputnik fell off in a heap next to the machine, but Jason's foot caught beneath it.

He struggled frantically to get his shoe out from under the weight. Sputnik yowled and scrambled from Jason's sweatshirt to hide under the tree.

The helicopter loomed closer, now a giant black beetle about to pounce on the tiny figures. As it cleared the hill behind them, Jason's foot popped out.

"Quick!" he cried to Edna, who seemed to be mesmerized by the sound of the helicopter. "We've got to get it under the tree!" His voice jolted her out of her trance, and together they wrestled the cycle into the shelter of the branches.

They huddled against the trunk, Jason holding Sputnik in his arms. The helicopter roared overhead, bright lights searching the landscape, probing into the branches of the scrawny tree. Jason could hear the crackle of radio conversations coming down from the open side door. Then, as if in slow motion, the helicopter moved toward the hills beyond. Jason exhaled. His palms were sweaty, and his heart felt as if it would burst out of his body.

He moved his foot, which was still hurting from being crushed under the cycle, and was about to stand up, when he heard the helicopter rotor again. It was coming back. Jason and Edna froze against the trunk of the tree, forgetting Sputnik in their fear. Edna looked up through the branches as the giant helicopter hovered above, its propeller kicking up a cloud of dust, its spotlight shining straight down.

Jason looked down. *Sputnik!* The cat, seemingly delirious, staggered out from under the tree toward the light from the helicopter. He lunged and grabbed Sputnik's tail just as he reached the edge of the circle of light, gathering the wild-eyed cat into his arms. After what seemed like a long time, the helicopter sped back toward the base.

Had it seen them? Jason wondered. Was there a giant net about to be thrown over them, snaring them in a trap? Maybe the black plane was from the government also?

Edna let out a sigh as she sat up. She seemed unfazed by the close call. Jason wondered if she really understood how much danger they were in. They crept out from under the tree and sat on the ground next to the cycle.

"That reminds me," said Edna, brushing pine needles out of her hair. She looked up at the sky, and then pointed at a star directly above them. "See that big blue star?"

"Yeah."

"That's Vega. One time Sam and I went to one of its inner planets for a sightseeing vacation. One week, all expenses paid. We were looking for giant purple ploppy flowers when this hairy snarkle about eight feet tall, with four eyes and VLT, came roaring out of the jungle."

"VLT?"

"Very large teeth. Was he hungry! Big slobbery lips, teeth sharp as razors. Sam had forgotten the ray gun, so we had to scram, with the snarkle slobbering and gnashing his teeth right behind. Almost caught us, too. Crawled under a rock just in time. He came so close you could smell his breath. Snarkle breath is not something you want to smell more than once in a lifetime. How's that foot?"

"It's okay."

Edna looked at Jason. "Hurts, doesn't it?"

Carefully she took off Jason's shoe and sock.

"Might think about changing the old socks once in a while, kid," she said, wrinkling her nose.

Edna slowly rubbed her hands together and then held Jason's bare foot in them. At first Jason felt nothing, but then his foot felt warm, as if tiny sparks of heat were soothing his ankle. Slowly she took her hands away, and Jason could see a faint blue light coming out of her palms. The pain seemed to melt away, and he put his sock and shoe back on and stood up.

"It doesn't hurt anymore. How do you—"

"Earthlings don't know how to do that?"

"No one I've met. And Berkeley would be the place to meet people who could make blue healing light come out of their hands."

Edna smiled. "When we get back to your house, we can work on the cat. Cats take a little more time to fix than feet."

ason and Edna piled back on the cycle, with Sputnik once more zipped up in Jason's sweatshirt. By now the cat's head was limp, as if Sputnik had no more energy even to hold his head up.

"It's okay, Sputs, it's okay," said Jason, stroking his moist head.

The cycle rose straight up, hovered for a moment, and then headed toward the hills to the east, over a vast stretch of empty desert. Jason kept turning to look behind them, trying to see if the black helicopters were once more on their tail. Or the dark plane. In the distance in front of them a highway stretched straight in both directions, perpendicular to the direction they were flying. A small building stood next to the highway, with a neon sign in front.

"Is Sam down there?" asked Jason.

"No, he's farther away," said Edna. "Beyond that building. I can see the blip on the screen. Are we still in Area 51?"

"I hope not."

They flew over the little building on the highway and into the desert, flat to the horizon, white in the moonlight. The rocket cycle purred across the sky as Edna and Jason looked intently for any sign of life.

"There!" Below them was a tiny black shape in the midst of the emptiness. Edna slowed the cycle and they descended.

The Dart stood by itself on the empty desert floor. Edna landed the cycle and they got off and walked toward the car, gleaming in the moonlight. Except for a long scorch mark on one side, it looked untouched. Jason took off his helmet and reached out to touch the Dart's hood, still warm from the daytime heat. The interior was dark, shaded from the moonlight.

Sputnik meowed weakly from his perch in Jason's sweatshirt. Jason lifted him out and laid him on the hood of the Dart, then peered in the open driver's window.

"Ah!" With a start he jumped back. "Where's the flashlight?"

Edna rummaged in her purse. "Here!"

She clutched Jason's arm as he shone the light into the car. There, lying on the front seat, was Sam.

Slowly Jason pulled the door open. Edna leaned in and called softly, "Sam!" And again, "Sam, it's us!" The figure on the seat didn't move. "Honey, wake up. We've come to take you home."

Sam was still.

Jason remembered that in an emergency you should take someone's pulse. He reached for Sam's arm. Gently he held the small wrist, tips of his fingers searching for a sign of life. There was nothing.

He took a deep breath.

Then, almost like the ghost of a pulse, he felt a slight movement in the wrist. "He's alive!"

Edna leaned closer. "Sam, come back. Wake up, Sam." His lips were parched and his face sweaty, hair tousled. Edna pulled herself out of the car and began to rummage intently in her purse, throwing out a bar of soap, a feather duster, a blue lipstick, a can of shoe polish, the chain for the rocket cycle, and what looked like a small toaster.

"Aha!" she said at last, holding up a tiny blue bottle. "Smelling salts." She uncorked the bottle and leaned back into the car, holding the open bottle next to Sam's nose. He shivered and let out a small sigh.

"Gimme that bottle of water you brought," she said. "He won't last long without water in this heat."

Jason reached into his sweatshirt. "It's gone! Must've fallen out over the desert."

They searched all through the Dart, but there was no water. Only an empty bottle and a few papers in the glove compartment along with Sam's ray gun.

Edna muttered, "What good's that ray gun anyway? Can't make water, can't even make coffee. You'll have to fly the cycle back to that place we saw on the highway."

She started walking toward the cycle.

Jason, following behind, said, "Me? I don't know how to drive." This seemed like an impossible idea. He had never driven a car, much less a rocket cycle. You had to be fifteen to even start learning how to drive a car.

"You'll pick it up. I've got to stay here with Sam. And if you meet someone out there, it would be better to talk earthling to earthling."

"I can't even drive a car—I mean, I've never done anything like that," said Jason.

Edna stopped and turned, looking intently at him, her eyes glittering in the moonlight. "I *know* you can do it."

"But I don't—it's just that—" Jason heard himself whining. He stopped and stared out across the desert. Maybe Edna was right. Maybe you could do things that seemed impossible at first. Jason looked at her. "Okay, I'll try it. But only on the ground. No flying." He strapped his helmet on.

"That's more like it, kid." She turned and walked to the cycle. "Remember, try to keep it going—don't let it die. First thing is, the rocket cycle isn't like your Earth cycles. It's got a pedal for the gas and one for the brakes. The handlebars are just for turning and going up and down when you're flying. Simple."

Jason climbed on the cycle. "Sputs, you stay here. I'll be right back."

The rocket cycle was smaller than a regular motorcycle, but now that he was straddling the seat, it seemed huge and complicated. His arms stretched to reach the handlebars. Edna leaned over and started the engine.

"Give it a little gas," she said. The cycle didn't move. "That's the brakes. Try the pedal on the other side."

Jason pushed down on the gas pedal. The cycle jumped ahead, then stopped. He struggled to keep his sweaty hands on the grips.

"Keep your foot pressed down. If you're going to fly, get it going good on the ground and then pull up on the handlebars."

"No way I'm going to fly," said Jason.

"Suit yourself, but you could do that, too."

"I can't even drive this thing on the ground," said Jason as he pushed down again on the gas, trying to keep his foot steady. Once more the cycle leaped forward, then stopped. Again the gas, again it stopped.

Stop.

Start.

Stop.

Start.

Would he ever get it right?

"You'll get it, kid, you'll get it," said Edna encouragingly.

He pushed harder on the gas pedal and—*BLAM!*—the cycle jumped forward, nearly sending him flying, like a bucking bronco trying to throw a cowboy. Before he had time to think, he was roaring across the desert at a terrifying speed, gripping the handlebars with all his strength, his foot tensely on the gas pedal. He could feel sweat running down his neck and the loudness of the rocket cycle blasting in his ears. The cycle bounced as it ran across the desert, and the clatter of the wheels on the desert floor vibrated the handlebars. The wind whipped his face, but to Jason's amazement, nothing went wrong. He didn't crash, and he didn't lose control. After all, he thought, maybe if he didn't fly but just drove with the cycle on the ground, that was something he *could* do.

He was glad he wasn't learning how to drive the rocket cycle in the middle of Berkeley. Then he would have had to go straight down the street, stop at stoplights, not hit cars, not drive on the sidewalk, not go too fast, not run over squirrels.

The desert was empty in every direction. If the cycle tottered one way or the other as it roared along the desert floor, it didn't matter, and if he went too fast or too slow, or stopped and started clumsily, or fell over and landed in a heap on the ground, there was no one there to see it and laugh at him. It was Jason and the

Zarathustra 2001 under the stars, wobbling their way through the desert.

Slowly, he got the hang of driving the cycle and began to enjoy it, the warm desert air blowing in his face, the engine roaring as he pushed the gas pedal. The land stretched flat in front of him and he began to accelerate. He tried turning the handlebars side to side, and started doing huge circles, around and around, clouds of dirt flying up behind the cycle. Then figure eights, leaning into the corners and gunning the engine.

Suddenly he thought, Where am I? What am I doing, going around in circles while Sam is dying of thirst?

He saw a long gully sunken into the desert floor in front of him. It stretched far into the distance on either side. Had they seen this as they flew to the Dart? He screeched to a stop at the edge of the deep, wide chasm, got off the cycle, and peered down. It was too wide to jump over and too steep to ride down into. All around was the night sky and an endless flat land. The moon was straight above, casting a ghostly light. He peered into the distance in every direction, but there were no lights. Where was he? Where was the highway?

He realized that in his excitement at being able to ride the rocket cycle, he had gotten completely lost.

Twenty-Seven

Somewhere inside, Jason knew what he had to do, but another part of him rebelled at the thought.

No way, he said to himself. No way. I can't fly this thing. What if the engine stalls? What if I run out of gas five thousand feet in the air? What if it's more compli-cated to fly than Edna said?

She and Sam were always making things sound easier than they turned out to be. Then again, what choice did he have? He was lost in the desert, and flying was the only way to find out where he was. He had to help Sam. He had figured out how to drive the cycle on land—now he would learn to fly it through the air. Edna's words resounded in his head: "I *know* you can do it."

Jason climbed back onto the cycle, steered it away from the creek bed, and accelerated out onto the flat desert.

"I can do it I can do it I can do it," he muttered over and over.

Slowly, carefully, he pulled up on the handlebars. Soundlessly and seemingly without effort, the cycle rose into the air. He held the handlebars as steady as he could, unnerved to be high in the air so quickly on a machine he hardly knew how to control. But sooner than he had on the ground, Jason began to feel comfortable flying. The rocket cycle seemed happier in the air, too, like a bird that had been held in a cage and now could fly free.

Jason looked at the landscape below him, a desert surrounded by rocky mountains. He saw that his fears had been right: He had gone in the wrong direction. Far away, at the edge of the horizon, in the opposite direction from where he thought it was, he saw the light of the building next to the highway. He swung the cycle around in a big arc and steered toward the light. Soon it was below him, a small diner in the middle of the desert, its front lit by a neon sign: ROSIE'S DESERT CAFÉ AND HAIR SALON.

Below it, there was a smaller hand-lettered sign: LAST GAS FOR 50 MILES.

In front of the diner stood a rusted gas pump.

The two-lane highway was empty. Far down the road to the north were the lights of a small town. Below him, a country music song drifted out of the open door of the diner: "Trailers for sale or rent,/Rooms to let fifty cents. . . ."

The parking places in front of the diner were empty, but an old pickup stood by the back door. The diner's lights were still on.

He circled around once, then again, high in the air, looking down.

He would have to land. That seemed much more complicated than taking off, but there was no way around it. Zarathustra would have to come back to Earth.

As he tilted the cycle forward and eased off the gas, the engine faltered and the rocket cycle headed straight down at the diner, coughing and sputtering. Jason yanked back on the handlebars, but it was too late. The cycle knocked the antenna off the diner, teetered at the edge of the low roof, and flipped over, landing among the garbage cans in back. Jason groaned and slowly pulled himself out. He was amazed to find that, aside from a torn pant leg and a small scratch on his hand, he was unhurt. He pulled the cycle out from under the cans and inspected it. Would it fly again?

As he was taking off his helmet, the back door of the diner opened. "What's going on out here?"

A woman with blond hair done up in a bun stood in the doorway, a cigarette in her hand, a dish towel over her shoulder. "Mister, don'tcha know how to park? Had too much to drink?"

She stepped closer to Jason. Her eyes opened wide. She put out her cigarette and leaned over to inspect him in the dim light.

"Wait a minute, here," she said, pointing at the rocket cycle. "Aren't you a little young to be driving that thing?"

A list appeared in Jason's mind. He could say that he was:

1. a midget, or
2. had a special permit, or
3. his mother let him drive the Zarathustra late at night, or
4. he needed to get some water for a pair of aliens whose spaceship had broken down in the middle of the desert.

He knew that whatever he said would sound strange, number 4 most of all, especially while standing in back of Rosie's Desert Café and Hair Salon in the middle of the night, miles from anywhere. He decided to try the direct route: "Have you got any water?"

The woman stood back and opened the door for Jason, shaking her head. "Kids these days. . . ." Then she introduced herself. "Come on in. I'm Rosie."

Jason looked up at her, and said, "Hi, I'm Joey," thinking it might be better somehow if she didn't know his real name.

Inside the café it was cozy—country music was playing on the radio, a few worn but immaculate Formica tables with little packets of sugar and ketchup and mustard on them stood near the windows, and a long, polished countertop ran along the back wall. Off to the side, behind a folding screen, he caught a glimpse of a few hair dryers and cans of hair spray and gel, combs, and scissors. Tacked to the wall were posters of people posing in long-ago-glamorous hairstyles.

He sat at the counter.

"Thirsty, huh?" said Rosie, looking intently at him. She put a glass of water on the counter. "I was getting ready to close up."

Jason drank the water in big gulps. When he finished, he set the glass back on the counter and burped. "Do you have a bathroom?"

"Out in back, around the corner." The woman was again looking intently at him and seemed to be turning an idea over in her mind. Jason avoided her gaze as he went outside to find the bathroom. Opening the door on his way back in, he heard her talking softly into the telephone behind the counter. He stopped to listen in the doorway, out of her view.

"Yes, Officer, there's something a little odd about this. He looks like a nice kid, but—Maybe you should come out and—" Just then, she turned around. Jason pretended to be opening the door. Quickly she hung up the phone.

"Something to eat?" she asked, smiling.

His mind was racing. Was a policeman speeding toward the café, with siren wailing and lights flashing, to arrest him as a runaway and send him back to Berkeley? What would Sam and Edna do?

"No, that's okay, I should be going. Do you have any bottled water?"

"Sure, a couple of bottles in the fridge. Sure you won't have a bite? I cook a mean hamburger."

His mouth began to water as she threw a hamburger on the griddle. It smelled scrumptious. Why couldn't she cook it faster? Why did hamburgers have to taste so good? Before he knew what he was saying, he blurted out, "Could you make it a cheeseburger?"

"Sure. So, whatcha doin' out here in the middle of Nevada?"

"Uh . . . family trip . . . a little fun in Las Vegas." His voice trailed off as he looked through the window. No police car.

"Las Vegas, huh? Vegas is about a hundred miles thataway."

"Oh."

After what seemed like an eternity, she slid the scrumptious-looking cheeseburger across the counter. As Jason squeezed a package of ketchup on it, he thought of the Dart. Maybe the dust drive had broken again. Maybe that was why it was stuck in the desert. He took a big bite out of the burger.

When Rosie turned away, he grabbed as many packets of ketchup as he could and stuffed them in his pocket. He picked up the cheeseburger again, but just as he was taking another bite, he heard a car outside. No siren. No flashing light, but a police car for sure. Jason tried to pretend that he hadn't noticed.

Rosie went to the front door. "I'll be back in a sec."

His heart pounding as Rosie stepped outside to talk to the police, Jason knew it was his only chance. He put down the half-eaten cheeseburger, lunged across the counter, and opened the refrigerator door, grabbing two bottles of water and stuffing them down his shirt. He rolled off the counter and scrambled for the back door, helmet in hand, just as the policemen came in the front. They dashed after him, yelling.

Jason slammed the back door shut and pushed a garbage can against it, then dragged the cycle away from the café and frantically started it up.

The cycle roared as he stepped on the gas, sending a cloud of dust into the faces of the policemen as they fell out the door. He cornered the rocket cycle around the café and out onto the road.

No time for a helmet now, he thought, tossing it to the side of the road.

The rocket cycle made a mad dash down the highway—Jason hardly knew which direction he was going. The police car followed, getting closer and closer, lights flashing, siren wailing.

One of the policemen came on the loudspeaker. "PULL YOUR VEHICLE TO THE SIDE OF THE ROAD, YOUNG MAN!"

Jason wavered, his mind racing. Should he give up? It would be a simple thing to do; maybe the policemen could help him.

The loudspeaker blared again: "PULL TO THE SIDE OF THE ROAD IMMEDIATELY!"

Jason hesitated. He thought of Sam and Edna in the desert with a feverish Sputnik and a broken-down Dart. It would be a disaster to let anyone know about them, stranded out there. It would be the end. They would never get home if the government captured them. He had to take care of them. Jason glanced behind again, then pushed hard on the gas pedal. Though the rocket cycle roared ahead, the police seemed to be able to follow its every move. No matter what Jason did, the cruiser was right behind.

In desperation he bounced off the highway and into the desert—surely the police wouldn't be able to follow on the rough ground. But the police car screeched off the road and was soon closer than before, careening over the desert, the officers inside grimacing as they kept him in their headlights. They were drawing closer.

Suddenly, in the midst of the noise and the sirens and the dust and the police spotlight, Jason heard himself saying out loud, "DUHHH!" And then, "How could I have forgotten?"

Slowly, carefully, he pulled back on the handlebars. With a majestic inevitability, the rocket cycle rose into the sky. Far below, the police car slowed and came to a stop, its headlights shining at nothing.

Jason was far above them now. He was free. He was beyond the reach of the Earth, halfway to the stars. Officers Jones and Mattingly, two of the Nevada Highway Patrol's finest, jumped out of their car, guns drawn. There was nothing they could do but stand helplessly looking up at the tiny blip disappearing into the night sky.

"I've seen strange things out here," said Officer Mattingly, shaking his head, "but that is definitely the strangest."

He leaned back in the cruiser and radioed to headquarters. "Mattingly here. Say, you're not going to believe this. . . ."

Twenty-Eight

As he glided across the sky, Jason felt as if he were at the top of a great dome of the night, the glittering stars scattered like tinsel from horizon to horizon. The air was cool on his face and the moonlight bathed the rocket cycle.

He was elated. He could fly, and his worries were gone. No matter what obstacles came his way, they would be easy to handle. The wind was in his hair, the Zarathustra rumbled reassuringly beneath him as he floated back to the little spaceship in the middle of the desert.

Soon the Dart was below him.

He peered down, looking for Edna to wave up.

But there on the desert floor, parked not far from the Dart, was the black plane that had been following them. Next to the car, two figures leaned over a third, who lay prone on the ground. It looked like Edna.

Jason's heart was in his throat, his mind racing. Who were they? Should he land? Fly back to Berkeley for help? Who could he trust?

Jason had never felt so alone.

But no matter who was down there, he had to face them. There was nothing else to do. He circled once and landed a little distance away, then walked slowly toward the car, his heart pounding.

The two figures stood near the Dart, black shapes against the moonscape of the desert, their faces hidden in shadow. The one in front, who was bald and short, spoke.

"Jason, I'm so glad we got here in time."

That hint of an accent.

Zimburger.

The bigger man behind took off his hat and smiled—a gold tooth glinted in the moonlight. Oddjob.

"What are you doing here?"

Zimburger extended his clammy hand.

"We thought you might be in trouble. I came to help you."

Jason had the urge to yell "YOU DID NOT!" but he

held his tongue. Oddjob smiled again and cracked his knuckles.

Behind Zimburger, Jason could see Edna lying on the ground, not moving.

"What happened to Edna?"

"A little accident, Jason, unavoidable."

"What did you do to her? Did you do something to Sam, too?" His voice was desperate as he backed away from the doctor.

"Jason, let me explain. After our little session I wasn't sure that your story was true. I hear many such stories, and for the most part they are fabrications, fantasies. For some reason—I don't quite know why—I decided to investigate your tale. I'm sorry if you found my methods devious. I soon discovered that, as you had told me, the aliens and their vehicle were genuine. You didn't make it up, did you? The real deal." His voice rose. "I never thought the day would come. Never. But now, after so many years"—his teeth were clenched —"I *know* UFOs are real." He banged his fist down on the hood of the Dart.

Hey, watch it, thought Jason, that's my buddy Sam's spaceship.

The doctor hesitated and then spoke in a soothing voice. "Of course my first thought was for your safety. I had to make sure that nothing would happen to you."

"Happen to me?"

Dr. Zimburger took off his hat and wiped the sweat

from his face. "These aliens may not be as benign as you think. Using Navy surplus guidance equipment, my cohorts and I were able to remotely take over the Dart's guidance system as it came in from outer space and direct it to the desert, thus saving San Francisco from a possible alien invasion."

"Alien invasion?" said Jason. "Sam and Edna and a 1960 Dodge Dart?"

The doctor seemed not to be listening. "When we lost the Dart on our radar, I was able to follow you and the alien woman here. Now I am afraid that I must take the car and the two aliens away to a facility, shall we say, where they will be kept safe and studied for the benefit of mankind. Of course all of this will be kept very quiet."

"Do you work for the government? Are you one of those CIA guys who finds aliens?"

"In a manner of speaking, yes, you could say so."

"Where's your accent from?"

Zimburger's cheek twitched.

"I was raised in a little Polish suburb of Philadelphia. Everyone around me spoke Polish, you see, and that's how I got this little accent. Haha."

Before he knew what he was saying, Jason blurted out, "What river did Washington cross during the Revolution?"

"River? Well, let's see, that must have been the, uh, the . . ."

Jason could see Sam still unconscious in the front seat of the Dart and Sputnik draped across the back seat like a wilted tortilla. Had Zimburger done something to them also? Jason backed slowly around the car, and when he came to the passenger-side window, he reached into the glove compartment and pulled out the ray gun. Its complex metal surfaces sparkled in the moonlight, and it vibrated slightly in his hand. The purple trigger shimmered.

He pointed it at the doctor. "Where are you from?"

Zimburger smiled his crooked smile. Oddjob, standing next to him, cracked his knuckles again. The wind blew gently across the desert, and the moon was directly overhead.

"Really, Jason, this isn't necessary. I'm sure we can work this out. I can explain everything."

The sound of a big rig shifting gears came from far away across the desert. Jason thought he heard Edna move. He turned his head slightly to listen.

Oddjob grabbed for the ray gun. Jason yanked it back, and it went off. A cloud of green miasma shot from the barrel, covering Oddjob with something that looked like murky lime Jell-O. The Jell-O quivered for a moment and then turned transparent and faded away.

Jason and Zimburger stared, their eyes wide open.

Oddjob was gone.

What have I done? thought Jason. He looked down at the spot where Oddjob had been.

A large toad sat placidly on the ground, pumping his throat in and out, as toads do.

"You've turned my brother Boris into a reptile," cried Zimburger, kneeling down.

So his name was Boris, thought Jason. And now he was a toad.

Boris the toad.

Jason held the gun up in the moonlight and saw that it was set to "Stun toads." It didn't say anything about "turn large bad person into toad," but apparently that was what had happened.

Zimburger was tenderly holding up Boris the toad.

"We had it all planned, Boris. Take the aliens back to Zimbovia, you and I. We would open a museum, show them off, put the Dart on display, make a lot of money. It would be like the old days. We could find pretty wives and dance the polka on Saturday nights. We would help Zimbovia rise from the ashes. But now I will have to go on alone."

He turned toward Jason. "Would it really be so bad to take these aliens to Zimbovia for the betterment of mankind? Would it? They might be somewhat incapacitated after my experiments, but is that such a great price to pay? To make my little country great again?"

"But your country doesn't exist. It disappeared in 1982."

Zimburger's nostrils flared. "That is not true! Zimbovia will never die." He put his fist over his chest. "It will always live in our hearts. But you, you had to ruin it all by turning my brother into a toad with that stupid little, little . . ."

"I didn't mean to do it."

Zimburger stared at the ray gun like a zombie, not seeming to care that it was aimed at him. He stood up and moved toward Jason, backing him around the car. Would the ray gun fire again? wondered Jason. Did he want to turn somebody else into a toad? Even if that somebody was a crazy psychologist?

Zimburger was drawing closer. He lunged for the gun, and Jason lurched backward, tripping over Edna's seemingly lifeless body. The ray gun flew out of his hand, and the doctor dove for it. Before Jason could reach it, Zimburger had it trained on him.

"Ha, pipsqueak! Now I'm in the driver's seat, huh?" He turned the ray gun over and read the settings on the dial:

"'Temp. vaporize, Mushymooshy, Cook oatmeal.' Ha! 'Cook oatmeal'? Who wants to cook oatmeal? I hate oatmeal. 'Stun toads' . . . poor Boris."

He trained the gun on Jason. "Prepare to be a toad, my friend!"

Jason stood frozen in fear.

But then the doctor glanced down at the ray gun and read the last setting on the dial: "'CREATE UNIVERSE'?" He looked at Jason. "Does this really work?"

"I don't know. I never tried it."

The doctor began dancing and waving the ray gun in the air, his shoes kicking the dust up. "You can't fool me," he cried. "I know it's real. I know it."

He turned his face up to the moon. "Create universe! For twenty years I have been waiting to find something like this." He began to laugh a maniacal laugh, laughing so hard that he started coughing. As he bent over to catch his breath, Jason leaped for the ray gun, but Zimburger pulled it back.

"Ha, pipsqueak! Think you can fool me? No chance, kid, this guy is about to rule the world. *This* funky universe will disappear when I create my own! *My* universe will obliterate this paltry piffle of overstuffed rocks and dirt and microwave ovens and bad poetry. I hate poetry. POOF! Gone forever."

He spread his arms wide, sweat dripping from his face. "I can see it up in lights—'Coming soon'"—he flung his hand in an arc above his head—"'Zimburger Universe'!"

Wacko, thought Jason. A complete nut job.

Slowly Zimburger's arms fell to his sides. He stood staring into the distance for a long time. Then, with a feverish look in his eyes, he carefully changed the setting on the ray gun and pointed it at Jason.

What is it set on? thought Jason, desperately.

"Are you ready, my friend?"

Jason felt as if he was outside his body. There was a roaring in his ears, and his knees quivered. He was standing by Edna's feet, and right behind Edna was Sam in the Dart.

Well, at least we'll all go together, he thought. Sam and Edna and me.

Suddenly he felt Edna's shoe tapping gently on the side of his sneaker. She was awake! Alive! Next to her lay her purse with its infinite hidden possibilities. Jason began to edge around the hood of the Dart.

Summoning his courage, he smiled at Zimburger. "I know where there are lots more ray guns, with lots of other things you can do." He was making it up as fast as he could. "Look in here." He pointed inside the passenger side of the Dart. Sam lay unconscious in the driver's seat.

"You don't fool me," said Zimburger. "And anyway, what more could I want now?"

"See for yourself," said Jason, backing away. "I'll stand over here"—he said this part loudly—"and you look in the glove compartment"—again loudly—"and see what you find."

Zimburger waved him away and nervously looked inside the car. "I don't see anything. Aside from the other alien."

"Keep looking. In the glove compartment. There are lots of ray guns in there."

Out of the corner of his eye, Jason saw Edna slowly rise. She tiptoed behind the Dart and climbed stealthily on top, purse in hand. While Zimburger leaned farther into the car, she pulled a large object like a frying pan out of her purse. Standing on top of the car, she raised the pan above Zimburger's backside.

His head still inside, he called out, "I don't see anything in this glove compartment."

He pulled his head out, and as he did so, Edna swung the frying pan.

KLONG!

Zimburger fell in a heap, the ray gun at his side. He was out cold.

"That'll teach that overgrown baby. What a nut job." Edna smiled at Jason. "Let's see, what terrible things did Zimburger think we were going to do to you? Hmm . . . maybe fry you in butter and eat you for lunch? No, thanks. I hate fried kid. By the way, where's the toad?"

Jason pointed to the spot, but Boris the toad had disappeared. They looked under the car and all around it.

"There," said Jason, pointing. Far out in the desert they could just make out Boris, hopping contentedly toward the mountains in the distance.

"Strange," said Edna. "Did you get the water? Sam's still really out of it."

They splashed water over Sam. His lids fluttered, then his eyes opened.

"Ooh, my head."

"Mine, too, honey," said Edna, standing back. "That was some drink those guys gave me."

"Guys? What guys? What am I doing here?" Sam stared groggily across the desert.

"I was wondering the same thing," said Edna. "We had a helluva time finding you."

Sam gulped down the bottle of water.

"I was coming in good over Berkeley. . . ." He scratched the back of his neck. "Then something happened and I couldn't control the steering. I must've conked out. Next thing I know, I'm broiling in the desert with no water." He looked over at Zimburger's plane. "Where did that come from?"

"Long story," said Jason. "I'll tell you about it later." He smiled at Sam in the moonlight. He was alive. Jason felt a wave of relief sweep over him.

"And who's this?" said Sam, almost tripping over the doctor.

"Dr. Zimburger," said Jason. "Not-nice guy. And crazy, too. I'll tell you about it later."

The doctor was trying sleepily to get to his feet.

"We better tie him up," said Jason. "You never know what he might do."

The three of them pulled the doctor into the plane and tied him to the seat. His head lolling back and forth, he was drooling and muttering to himself, "I will rule the world! I will create a universe!"

"Create a universe?" said Sam. "How does he expect to do that?"

"You remember, it's that setting on the ray gun." Jason pulled out the ray gun and gingerly pointed.

"Oh, that," said Sam. "That doesn't do anything. It's a joke."

"A joke?"

"Yeah. Just a dinky light show. Watch."

He pointed the ray gun straight up and pulled the trigger. A glob of light shot into the air and exploded, sending a small spray of colors out into the night, like a cheap fireworks display. The colors fizzled into darkness.

"That's great," said Edna, "but not too brainy, Sam. We've got Area 51 just over the hill and black helicopters breathing down our necks and you're putting up a light show: 'Here we are! Come and get us!'"

"Oops."

Jason reached into the back seat through the window and stroked Sputnik's feverish head. "We've got to get this guy home."

Sam climbed into the driver's seat and flipped a series of switches, then pushed the starter button. Lights flickered across the dashboard, but the engine would not start.

"Quantum regulator," said Sam. "And probably that darn dust drive. Always gives me trouble. I should take it back to Orion and get a refund." He opened the hood and leaned into the engine, adjusting parts and tightening knobs, grunting. He straightened up. "Regulator's working fine now, but I was right, the dust drive is on the fritz, again. And I got no—"

Jason reached in his pocket and handed Sam the packages of ketchup.

"Where'd you get those?"

"Rosie's Diner. Great cheeseburgers. I'll tell you about it later."

Sam squeezed the ketchup, package by package, into the dust drive, throwing the empties on the ground. He slammed the hood shut: *Whump*.

From the west, like an echo, but much louder, came another *WHUMP!*

Two thin dark shapes were flying fast toward the Dart, very close to the ground.

"Duck!" cried Edna.

Jason huddled against the car. An enormous roar shook the ground as two swept-wing black jets streaked over the Dart, seemingly close enough to touch. Jason covered his ears and pressed his body against the Dart. The jets turned high in the sky and headed back for another pass.

"Could you fly a little closer, already?" yelled Edna, shaking her fist at the planes. Her voice was drowned out as the jets howled back over the Dart.

"Let's get out of here," said Sam.

"What about the rocket cycle?" said Jason.

"Have to leave it. Won't fit in the Dart. I'll come back later and get it."

"You can't leave it with Zimburger," said Jason.

"But it's my only . . ." Sam rubbed his chin, then

looked up. The black jets were headed back for another pass. He shook his head and walked to the rocket cycle, patted it gently, then set the ray gun on "Burn large hole." Standing back, he pointed the ray gun at the cycle. He held his other hand over his eyes and pulled the trigger. In a flash of flame and smoke, the cycle evaporated, leaving only a charred spot on the ground and the smell of burned rubber in the air. Without looking back, he walked to the Dart and climbed in with Jason. Edna sat in back with Sputnik.

"Gonna build me another one someday."

"You built it?" asked Jason.

The roar of the jets overhead drowned out Sam's reply.

Sam hardly seemed to notice the jets, engrossed in his own thoughts. He muttered a list as he flipped the switches on the dashboard: "Reactors . . . gravity rotators, amplifiers . . . anodes . . . charge lights one, two, three." Again he pushed the start button. The Dart rumbled to life.

"Hold on!"

"So long, Zimboolie," yelled Edna out the window at the doctor, who lolled in the plane, his eyes still crossed and his head rolling around on his shoulders. Sam steered the Dart in a wide arc on the desert floor and soon they were flying very fast toward the mountains.

"Jets to the left!" cried Jason. Sam banked sharply away and toward the nearby mountains. Jason looked down and saw Zimburger's plane, alone in the empty landscape.

Soon the Dart was racing into a rocky valley. Sam strained forward in the front seat, trying to see the terrain ahead. "Did we lose them?"

Jason looked back. At first he couldn't see anything in the gloom, but then he made out the shapes of the jets, curling up the valley behind the Dart.

"No."

Edna spoke up from the back. "Remind me, Sam— why do we keep coming back to this blasted planet? I've been to a lot of planets in my time, but this is the only one where they put you in jail for being a tourist."

BZZZZZZTTTT!

A blast of energy shot out from under one of the jets and hit the Dart. Sputnik's eyes popped open and he yowled as sparks crackled across his fur. He jumped straight up and ran around in circles, eyes wild with electricity, then just as suddenly collapsed back in a feverish heap on the seat.

"That does it," cried Edna, shaking her fist at the jets out the back window. "Could you hand me that ray gun, kid?"

Edna rolled down her window, the wind rushing into the car. Taking the ray gun, she leaned out and pointed it at the jet below them. As she pulled the trigger, all the colors of "Create universe" flashed out from the gun and enveloped the jet, which seemed to hesitate as if surprised, then turned and fell away in a wide arc. Edna leaned farther out, trying to aim at the other jet, but it too peeled away, only to return as soon as Edna had put her head back into the car.

"Nice shot," said Jason. "I mean, for a grandmotherly type."

Edna laughed. "That'll show them," she said, rolling up the window and handing the ray gun back to Jason.

Sam shook his head. "Gotta lose these guys somehow."

The Dart sped up and out of the valley, and soon they were high above the desert, barely ahead of the two black shapes angling through the air. One of the jets darted forward, engines growling.

"He's right above us," cried Jason.

"The other one's underneath," said Sam. "Time for overdrive." He punched a button and the Dart jolted ahead, leaving the jets behind. "That'll keep them off our tail for a little bit. Honey, is there a cardboard box by your feet?"

"Yes."

"Could you pass it up, quick?"

Jason took the dusty box and opened it. Inside, a tangle of wires was loosely wrapped around a green metal canister.

"Teleporter," Sam said. "Picked it up at a surplus store in Andromeda."

"What does It do?"

"Takes you somewhere else, lock, stock, and barrel. Directions are in the box."

"This is all there is." Jason held up a piece of paper. "It's for emergencies."

Edna leaned forward from the back seat. "I think this qualifies."

"I think that wire goes in there." Sam pointed at a socket in the dashboard.

TELEPORTER

RANDOM SHORT RANGE SINGLE USE

NONDIRECTIONAL DEVICE

RANGE: 100 TO 2000 KILOMETERS

WARNING!
Nondirectional Device:
YOU HAVE NO CONTROL OVER DESTINATION!

FOR EMERGENCY USE ONLY.

Mfd. by Deus ex Machina Productions, Inc.
All Rights Reserved

CRACK! A jolt of electricity shot through Jason's hand.

"Try that one instead," Sam said. "Then the blue one there, and the red one in the cigarette lighter."

The green light on top of the box started blinking. Below it was a black switch.

Jason fingered the switch nervously. "What should I do now?"

Edna leaned forward again. "Well, you could sit and twiddle your thumbs. But considering that those jets are back . . ."

Jason could feel the roar above them.

"And they're about to force us to crash-land in the desert, or worse, now might be a good time to see what's what, so to speak."

A teleporter? thought Jason. Where would it take them? How could it possibly work? His fingers were frozen on the switch.

Just then, the Dart lurched and seemed to be held immobile. Sam frantically turned the steering wheel back and forth. "Nothing," he cried. "No steering, no acceleration. Some kind of energy lock. Taking control of the Dart, gonna haul us in."

Edna said softly, "Sometimes in life, kid, you gotta go for it."

Jason took a deep breath and flipped the switch. At first, nothing happened. Then the box began to vibrate and the light on top turned red. The whole car shuddered, as if an electric charge was going through it.

As it had on the way to the bongo fish planet, the Dart started turning transparent. Jason could see the engine and all its inner workings. Then he could see all around the Dart, through the floors, the top, the seats. He looked up at the roof, and saw the black jet above. Then he began to see through his own hands and legs and feet. His sneakers glowed for a second and then disappeared. His jeans, his shirt, his belt, they were all going. He looked up through the roof at the jet roaring above and saw what was on the bottom of it:

USAF
SQUADRON 51-51
INTERGALACTIC ALIEN
IMMIGRATION AND
DETENTION SERVICE
"HERE TO SERVE YOU"

Alien detention? Sam and Edna? Just for being tourists? thought Jason.

" '*Here to serve you*'?" the almost-invisible Edna snorted. "Now I *know* this planet is—"

Suddenly there was a flash and a *POP!* and everything was gone.

No Jason, no Sam, no Edna, no Dart, just a great big huge enormous

Nothingness everywhere...

Poof! The Dart was gone, evaporated in a flash of blue light.

The black jets roared up and down and circled and hunted across the emptiness of the Nevada desert, like wolves whose prey had vanished. Their radar screens were blank, the desert empty, the moon shining down where an unidentified flying object used to be and was no more.

Slowly the jets turned and headed north to look for other prey, perhaps a small plane on the desert floor with a drooling therapist tied to its seat, a therapist whose briefcase contained stolen government UFO documents and other incriminating information.

Where the Dart had been, there was only a swirl of air, a rippling in the fabric of the cosmos, a breeze across the sand. The breeze rippled over the desert and sped away, drawn to the brightness of city lights, turning and twisting and floating on the teleportation express, the highway of the night, the instant 3-D message machine.

Jason floated calmly in this all-nothingness and everything-at-onceness. Flashes of color whizzed past, and there was a great roaring in his ears.

Then again, did he have ears? And where was poor Sputnik? he wondered, as he sped through the nothingness. Jason couldn't see his own body, but he could still conjure thoughts, and he found himself thinking, So this is teleportation. Now I know what it is. I'm in the middle of it.

He felt as if he should have been scared, but after everything that had happened to him, he was no longer afraid.

The nothingness rolled on and on for what seemed like a long time, though perhaps it was no time at all. Perhaps time itself had disappeared.

Then there was a *whoosh* and the clang of a bell, like the recess bell at school, and a puff of smoke, and all of a sudden he was in the Dart with Sam and Edna. He could feel the seat against his back again, and he could see the outlines of the windshield and the door next to him. He felt for his shirt and pants and belt. All there. He wiggled his toes, feeling his socks on the floor of the car. Where were his shoes? He looked down for them. Or was it up? Where his shoes should have been, they weren't. Gone. Missing. Not teleported.

Something else doesn't feel right, Jason thought sleepily, as if he was waking from a dream. A light was shining into the Dart, as if from above, but also not from above. Where was it coming from? Why did everything feel so strange, so upside down?

Meanwhile:

Far away, in Las Vegas, Nevada, Mr. and Mrs. Albert Ratootzi were walking down the street after a long night at the El Bimbo Casino. Suddenly, out of the empty sky, three pairs of shoes tumbled down, just missing Mrs. Ratootzi's large head and landing in a heap at her feet. Two of the pairs were purple high-top sneakers.

"Oh, my God!" cried Mrs. Ratootzi, looking up at the sky.

"Kids these days," muttered Mr. Ratootzi, kicking the shoes into the gutter.

Meanwhile #2:

Far away in the desert near Area 51, a psychologist with a beard was sitting on the ground next to a small plane, talking nervously to a group of dark-suited soldiers in flak jackets, their guns drawn, their heavy-duty flashlights aimed at him.

"It was the aliens, two of them, in a 1960 Dodge Dart from the Pleiades. They were blue and small and looked like someone's midget grandparents. One of them was named Edna, the other one was named Sam." He gave the soldiers a wild look. "You've got to believe me." He tugged at his beard. "They came with a kid. The kid had their ray gun. He turned my brother Boris into a toad. A big toad. But he's gone. He hopped away. He really did. I swear they turned him into a toad."

The soldiers smirked at one another, and one of them twirled his forefinger by his temple. He leaned over to the psychologist as another soldier fitted a straight-jacket on him. He spoke gently. "It's okay—everything is going to be okay. You'll be much happier in the state mental institution, you really will."

* * *

Out across the desert the large toad had hopped and hopped until he found a cleft in the rocks near the base of a mountain with a spring bubbling up from inside it, one of those rare pools in the desert that create a green-shaded world in the midst of the arid land, an oasis of peace and life and gurgling moisture. There the toad stopped in the moonlight. By now he had only the vaguest memory of his former life. He drank deeply and happily of the spring and then settled down to rest in the grass beside it, as the sound of the water flowing up from deep in the Earth soothed him to sleep.

There were other toads asleep near the spring, in their little homes in the Earth and the rocks, and they would become Boris's new family, his new home, his happy new life as a toad.

Maybe we're in heaven, thought Jason in his upside-down-no-shoes-almost-waking-up-from-teleportation dream state. He woke up a little more, and the answer came to him. Everything felt upside down because it *was* upside down, or rather the Dart was upside down, and Jason and Sam and Edna were hanging by their seat belts in the car. An acrid smell of smoke filled the air for a moment and then was gone. The Dart was gently rocking, and Jason and Sam and Edna swayed from side to side also, like a trio of bats in a cave.

There was a long silence, the only sound the swishing

of the wind outside the car. Then one by one, Sam and Jason and Edna started to giggle. Soon they were laughing uncontrollably but hardly knowing why. Everything seemed funny to them: The Dart was upside down, they had no idea where they were, they had escaped the terrible black jets. Everything was cause for merriment. Laughing, Sam tried to move the controls of the car, but nothing worked. He turned the steering wheel and pushed the gas pedal, but the Dart continued its gentle upside-down rocking. And in their happy state, none of them thought to look for Sputnik.

Upside-down Sam looked over at upside-down Jason. "No wonder that thing was so cheap. Teleports upside down! At least they got it half right."

"My shoes are gone," Jason said.

"Mine too," said Edna, looking down at her feet. Or rather up.

"At least we're somewhere else, aren't we?" said Sam.

"Somewhere-Else-Upside-Down!" said Edna from the back seat, laughing. "Say, what's that light, and all that smoky stuff outside? It looks like . . . like . . ." She stopped laughing and stared out the window of the Dart. "Wait a minute, here. I don't like the looks of this."

"The looks of what?"

"See that stuff outside the window? Some kind of smoke or vapors or something," said Edna.

Thirty

Sam and Edna and Jason stared out the windows of the Dart. "I think we're on an antimatter planet, where everything is upside down and the air is not too great either," said Edna, looking at the stuff swirling around the car.

"We couldn't possibly be on another planet," said Sam.

"Well, aren't we upside down? The teleporter probably malfunctioned. Now we're on some godforsaken antimatter planet a million light-years from home."

"I'm sure we're not that far away," Sam said.

"Great. We're only half a million light-years away? That's terrific."

Sam peered out the window. "Let's roll down the windows, see if we can hear anything."

"NO! It could be an ammonia atmosphere! One whiff and we're toast!" cried Edna.

Suddenly the front of the Dart started to rise up.

"Aaack!" cried Edna. "Who's controlling this thing? What's going on?"

Sam stared at the dashboard. "I think it's only—"

"Only antimatter aliens controlling the car, that's what," said Edna.

Lights flickered across the dashboard, and electrical surges crackled through the car's circuits.

The front of the Dart rose higher and higher, until the car was straight up and down.

At least Jason could sit with his back on the seat and the seat belt didn't dig into his shoulder.

"Now what, Sam?" cried Edna.

"I'm working on it," he said, pushing one button after another.

"I've heard about this kind of planet," said Edna. "The aliens take control of the spaceship and force it to their base station and then they suck your brains out and eat them. Or turn you into alien zombies."

"Oh, Edna," said Sam.

"Or maybe they'll dissect us piece by piece with those little instruments. That'll be really fun."

Jason looked outside. No sign of aliens, unless that whooshing noise far below came from other life-forms.

The car continued its rotation, the front slowly descending, until it was level and right side up.

"Okay. That's a start," said Edna.

"Maybe it's not an upside-down planet after all, huh?" said Sam, giving Edna a sideways glance.

Jason stared out the window. The orange mist still swirled around the car, turning red every few seconds, but it was starting to thin. He saw something orange and metallic emerging not far away. It grew clearer and clearer as Jason looked at it. It seemed very familiar.

All of a sudden, a delicious realization filled his mind, and he cried: "Sam! Edna! I know where we are!"

Thirty-One

Not far away, a peaceful ocean, covered by a blanket of fog, breathed like a sleeping giant, waves fluttering over its surface. Along the coast, the waves rolled in, one after another, watery fingers reaching out to the rocky shore.

Some of the waves rolled under a great bridge, to lose themselves in the waters of a large bay. Cars streamed across the bridge, their headlights piercing the mist.

At either end of the bridge, an enormous tower jutted up from the water, rising hundreds of feet into the air. Cables curved down from the two towers, and spotlights shone up from the roadway, lighting the bridge in a warm orange glow. On top of each tower a red warning light blinked on and off every few seconds.

Tonight the fog was thick and deep, hiding the bridge in a blanket that not even the towers pierced. If you had been looking down from the sky above just a few minutes earlier, you would have seen nothing of the bridge in the moonlight, only a rolling river of white cotton covering it and the waves rolling under it.

Then, out of the fog above the north tower, a swirling miasma of light would have appeared, a vortex of energy and transaerial potentiality. Out of the emptiness, at first like a puff of smoke and then more substantial, something shiny and green and rippling would have begun to take shape.

Something smooth and automotive.

Something at first transparent, then solid. At first upside down, then right side up. Something like . . . a lime-green 1960 Dodge Dart, rocking majestically in the spotlights of the great bridge.

Thirty-Two

Jason was laughing. He reached out and rolled down the car window.

"What are you doing?" cried Edna.

"I know where we are! We're not on another planet! See that big orange metal thing over there? That's the top of the Golden Gate Bridge! That's not ammonia outside! It's fog. Good old fog." Jason leaned out the window and spread his arms wide. "We're home."

He leaned back in and looked at Sam. "We're above the Golden Gate Bridge. Berkeley is right over there." He waved his arm in a half circle. "It's the bridge lights that make the fog turn orange." He laughed again. "Sputnik, we're home. We made it ba—" He turned to look in the back seat. "Sputnik? Where is he? Is he under the seat?"

"The cat?" said Edna. "He's . . . he's not here."

Jason's stomach churned. "Sam, where is he?"

"Got to be around here somewhere."

"Around here? Sam, we're above the Golden Gate Bridge." Jason leaned back on the seat and took a deep breath.

The fog receded beneath the Dart. They were alone in the moonlight above the blanket of white.

Edna leaned forward. "We'll find him, kid. He can't be too far away."

Jason felt like crying. After everything they had gone through, to come to this end and lose Sputs. It didn't seem fair.

Sam pressed the gas and the Dart moved forward, away from the tower. Slowly they descended, until they were just above the level of the fog. The Dart was carried along through trailers of mist, a traveler in a world of cotton and moonlight. Fog drifted past the windows, and the moonlight cast phantasmal shadows. The covering of white seemed to stretch on forever. Here and there, Jason could see signs of life below: a light, a radio tower, the Transamerica Pyramid. They were the only actors on a gigantic stage set made of clouds.

He recognized the dim glow of the lights through the fog at the Berkeley Marina and then the streetlights of

University Avenue stretching up to the hills. He strained to see over the hood of the Dart and could just make out San Pablo Avenue crossing University.

"Which way is home?" asked Sam.

"There," said Jason, pointing.

Sam brought the Dart down to the street and parked in front of Jason's apartment house. No one was around. Sam and Edna got out and stood on the sidewalk with Jason. Edna pulled him into a hug.

"We'll find him, kid. I know we will."

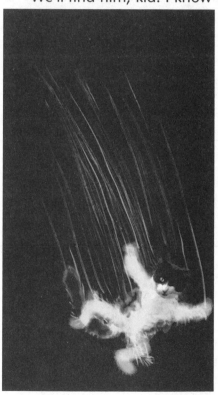

"Don't cats on Earth have nine lives or something?" said Sam.

Just then they heard a sound above them.

"A rocket!"

"A meteor!"

With a soft *whump,* the burning meteor—or whatever it was—crashed into Mrs. Sherbatskoy's hedge. The hedge sizzled and crackled, and then something fell out, tottered a few steps toward Jason, trailing wisps of smoke, and collapsed on the lawn.

"Sputnik!"

Jason picked the cat up and nuzzled close to him.

With Sam and Edna trailing behind, Jason carried Sputnik up the back fire escape and laid him on the bed in his room. The three of them stood looking down at the cat.

His eyes were wide-open and his feet were twitching. The fur had been burned off the end of his tail, and the rest of his coat was a tangle.

"He don't look too bad, considering he was a meteor," said Sam.

"C'mon, Sam, let's see if we can make this cat better," said Edna, and she rubbed her hands together, mumbling a few words in a strange language. She laid her hands on Sputnik, just as she had done with Jason's feet in the desert. "You can try it too, kid. Every bit helps."

He rubbed his hands together as Edna had, and then laid them on Sputnik. Sam did too.

At first nothing happened, and Jason could feel the weakness in Sputnik's body and hear his shallow breaths. Maybe he's too far gone, he thought.

"Cats are tough," said Edna. "All that fur or something."

Jason waited. His hands were starting to itch.

Then, slowly, a blue glow seemed to come out of

their hands. The smell of singed hair lingered, but Jason felt a tingling inside. He tried thinking about Sputnik, and it seemed easy. He felt the warmth of the cat's body in his hands next to Sam's and Edna's.

Jason closed his eyes and thought of Sputnik when he was little and had chased his tail round and round, when he had thrashed around in a paper bag, and when he had jumped off two flights of the back stairs and landed on his feet. He started feeling the happiness that the cat brought him. Sputnik was always around, like he was his best friend. Jason felt himself sinking deeper inside, and getting quieter. It seemed as if his heart was growing brighter, and warmer, and there was Sputs, as if inside, too. For a long time, the three figures huddled over the cat, but time didn't seem to matter, and Jason had no desire to move or get up.

Finally Jason opened his eyes. Sputnik was looking at him inquisitively. He twisted his nose and sneezed a little cat sneeze.

Sam and Edna opened their eyes and got up. They started walking around the room, and then began to dance with each other, smiling. The bedroom was filled with a mellow glow. Why does this make me feel so happy? Jason wondered. A memory bubbled up into his mind from when he was little, a memory of tiptoeing down the stairs late at night and peering into the living room, to see his parents dancing together, smiling at each other.

He thought about bongo fish dancing over that far-away lake, and as he drifted off to sleep, it was all mixed into one picture: Sam and Edna, his father and mother, bongo fish, and Sputnik, twirling around and around.

Jason woke to the bright sunlight of a late Sunday morning. He yawned and looked around the room. Sam and Edna were gone. At the foot of the bed sat Sputnik, staring at him. His mother stood in the doorway, smiling.

"Time to get up, sleepyhead," she said. "It's practically noon. Up late last night reading some adventure you couldn't put down?" She looked at the floor. "How did your sweatshirt get so dirty? And I can smell those socks from over here."

Jason lay back on the bed and smiled. "Big adventure, Mom, big adventure. . . ."

"I've got pancakes cooking. Hurry up before they get cold." She turned to Sputnik. "Well, look at Sputs, all bright-eyed and bushy-tailed. Doesn't he look better? But what happened to his tail?"

"Maybe he had a big adventure, too." Sputnik leaped across the bed and started licking Jason's face.

Thirty-Three

I t was breakfast time at Astro Joe's Space Camp in the Sierra foothills. The loudspeaker boomed out, "Jason Jameson to the main cabin! Your aunt and uncle are here to visit you."

Jason, with a forkful of instant scrambled eggs halfway to his mouth, turned and looked at his friend Nick. "Aunt and uncle? Why would my aunt and uncle visit me at camp on the Fourth of July?"

Nick shrugged his shoulders.

"And wait a minute. I don't *have* an aunt and uncle. I

mean there's Uncle Miltie, but Aunt Rose died, like, years ago."

"This sounds interesting," said Nick.

Astro Joe's wife, Mabel, was shuffling papers behind the counter as Jason and Nick walked in. She looked at the boys over her glasses and pointed across the room. Sitting placidly on a worn sofa reading magazines were Sam and Edna. They looked up at the boys with big smiles.

"Sam! Edna!"

Edna gave Jason a hug. "How ya doin', kid? Sam and me thought you might like to see some astronomical fireworks tonight." She turned to Nick. "You can come along, too. But, dang, you're just as skinny as Jason."

"Aww, Edna," said Sam.

Nick smiled. "Astronomical fireworks? Sounds goo—"

"We'll have some fine fireworks right here by the lake," interrupted Mabel from across the room. "Very safe. Most of them go at least six feet in the air. And I would have to get *permission* from Nick's parents for him to go *away* with you."

"Sure," said Edna heartily. "Call 'em up."

Mabel went into the office and they heard her talking on the phone. She came back after a few minutes.

"Just be sure to have the boys back by dinnertime to-morrow night," she said as she went back to shuffling her papers. "And by the way, how far will you be driving?"

"A ways down the road," said Sam, "down east a couple of parsecs or so, as the crow flies."

Mabel wasn't really listening as Sam said this, and so she missed the "parsecs" part, and even if she'd heard, she probably wouldn't have realized that a parsec, according to the dictionary, is *"a unit of astronomical length based on the distance from Earth at which stellar parallax is one second of arc and equal to 3.26 light-years, or 1.92×10^{13} miles."* Or, to put it more simply, 19,200,000,000,000 miles.

"Well, have a nice time and drive safely," said Mabel, as Sam and Edna walked out the front door, followed by Nick and Jason. As Jason passed Mabel at the counter, she leaned over to him and whispered, "Your aunt and uncle look a little bluish. Are they getting enough fresh veggies? You know, blueness can be a sign of creeping blasto-rotundalitis. Seaweed greens are really good for that."

Jason whispered out of the corner of his mouth, "Actually they suffer from a rare disease, acute Pleiadesitis. There's nothing that can be done for it. Except eating glazed doughnuts. That's the only thing that helps at all."

"Oh, dear," said Mabel, quickly retreating back to her papers.

They walked past the parking lot and into the field beyond, then through a thicket to where the Dart was hidden in a clearing, a small house trailer hooked behind it.

"Thought we'd camp on a little planet near Orion," said Sam. "They say it's going to be a great view of the supernova tonight."

"Camp on a planet?" said Nick.

"Yeah—say, Jason, does your friend here know anything about us?"

Jason looked at Nick. "Uh, no."

"Aww, that's okay," said Edna. "We can fill him in on the way."

"We should get going," said Sam. "We need to get the gollywhoggers cooking before sundown. Those giant Orion mosquitoes are a killer."

Nick turned to Jason and whispered, "Where's Orion? And what's a supernova? And what are gollywhoggers?"

Jason shrugged. He smiled at Nick. "You'll love gollywhoggers. They're delicious."

They all climbed into the Dart.

Nick looked at the dashboard, then sideways at Jason. "How fast does this car go?"

"Pretty fast," said Jason.

"Faster than a Corvette?"

"Definitely. And the view is *much* better."

"But what are we going to see?"

Jason smiled. "Who knows?"

Sam started the Dart. Lights flickered across the

dashboard as it rumbled to life. They drove out of the woods and onto the highway, and were soon tearing down the road at twice the speed limit. Jason opened his window and leaned out into the wind.

Sam looked around at the empty landscape. There were no cars on the road, no houses, only a few scrubby pines and empty hills rolling up to the mountains in the distance.

"Windows up! Hold on to your hats. Here we go." Sam pulled up on the steering wheel, and the Dart rose into the sky.

Jason saw Nick grab the door handle tightly, his knuckles white. He remembered (it seemed like long ago) sitting for the first time in Sam's car, more afraid than he had let himself admit. What was different now?

He leaned over and whispered, "Nervous?"

"A little."

Jason looked down at his own hands and then smiled at Nick. He said softly, "Sometimes in life you just gotta go for it."

Edna turned slightly from the front seat and winked at Jason.

Then they were flying straight up, faster and faster, the acceleration pushing them back hard against the seats. Soon they were above the mountains, past the clouds, past the stratosphere, and up into the deep blue-black of the highest atmosphere. Everything was quiet and they were out in space, the Earth below them, white clouds hugging the land beneath.

"W—W—WOW!" said Nick.

"Ohhh, it's so beautiful, isn't it?" said Edna.

Yes, thought Jason, as he looked at Sam and Edna. His eyes and his heart felt wide open, and everything looked strange and wonderful.

Edna smiled at him. "It's a big universe, kid, a big universe. And I know Elvis is somewhere in it. We'll find him someday, on some kind of bongo fishing trip."

Nick's face was pressed to the window. "Elvis?" He turned to look at Jason. "Elvis?" Jason shrugged his shoulders, and soon they all started laughing, for no reason at all, a million miles from anywhere.